HALLOWEEN HOMICIDE

KELLY HASHWAY

CONTENTS

To Ayla with love

Chapter One

The thing about fears is most people know they're irrational, but that doesn't make us any less afraid. Take horror movies for instance. We all know the things in the film can't hurt us, yet we jump when the killer comes on screen anyway. And if we hear a noise in the dark house while we're watching a scary movie, we somehow think the killer is inside our home. Our brains know it's not rational, but that doesn't stop our hearts from pounding or our pulses from racing.

I'm Dr. Sydney Warner, a psychologist with my own private practice. People tell me about their fears on a daily basis, and I have a few of my own as well. I've never used the token line, "The only thing to fear is fear itself," because telling someone that does nothing to alleviate their fears. It's like telling someone who is upset to calm down. It's futile.

Donna Barrett is sprawled out on the couch in my office, telling me how much she despises Halloween, which is only one week away. I know the real problem, which isn't her assertion that it's a holiday about kids begging for candy. She's afraid of a lot of things associated with this particular holiday. She's told me in previous sessions that she can't watch horror movies or any television shows about ghost hunters. She scares easily, which makes Halloween a trying time for her.

"I just don't see why teenagers have to go trick-or-treating. It's absurd. There comes a point where kids have to grow up and mature, and running around in costumes like they did when they were five is not the way to do it." Donna rests her arm across her eyes, and I have no doubt she's trying to block out mental images of trick-or-treaters from past years.

"Do you hand out candy each year?" I ask her. She could avoid the holiday by not participating. Most kids understand that if your front porch light isn't on, you're not handing out candy.

"It doesn't matter if I do or I don't. Hordes of kids march up and down my street. It's unnerving."

"Did you trick-or-treat as a child?" I ask.

"Never."

"Really? Why is that?" I have my pen poised over my notebook, ready to jot down what she says.

"I hated going inside costume shops. All those mechanical, creepy displays meant to jump out at you…" She shivers. "How is that fun?"

"Some people enjoy being scared because of the adrenaline rush," I say.

"Not me. I'm not a thrill seeker."

That much I'm well aware of.

"What about costumes themselves? Have you ever dressed up?" I cross my ankles, resting my notebook on my lap instead of the arm of the chair.

"Only once for an elementary school play I was forced to be in. I hated every second of it."

"What is it about costumes that bothers you?"

"People who need to hide behind masks are hiding something. That makes me uncomfortable."

"Were you hiding something when you were in the elementary school play?"

She removes her arm from her face and folds her hands on her stomach. "Yes. I was hiding how uncomfortable I was with everyone else pretending to be someone they weren't."

"Were your classmates scared?"

"No, they thought it was fun."

"And you can't see why someone might have fun dressing up in costume?" I ask.

To her credit, she doesn't answer right away. She's thinking it over. "I'm trying, Doc. I really am, but it just seems wrong to me."

I need to try another tactic. "Okay, forget costumes. Do you ever watch old movies?"

"Yes, I grew up watching them."

"And you enjoyed them?" I ask.

She nods.

"What time period would you say you like the clothing best?"

"I don't know. I suppose I liked Greta Garbo's outfits in *Anna Karenina*."

"That movie was from the 1930s, right?" I ask.

She nods. "What if someone dressed as Greta Garbo for Halloween? Would that be upsetting to you?"

Again, she pauses to consider this. "I suppose not, but I don't see kids doing that. They wouldn't even know who Greta Garbo is."

"You're probably right, but you do. What if you dressed as her?"

She immediately shakes her head. "I couldn't. I'm not going into a costume shop."

"What if I tracked down a costume for you?"

"Why?" she asks.

"I think it would be good for you to see the harmless fun of the holiday. You're viewing wearing a costume as a lie of sorts, but it's not if everyone knows the person wearing the costume is only doing it for fun."

She sits up and cocks her head at me.

"You're a fan of old movies and Greta Garbo. Well, she was an actress. She played parts, but that doesn't make her a bad person. She was an entertainer. Halloween is meant for entertainment. People enjoy dressing up and pretending to be something they aren't for the night."

"I could be Greta Garbo," she says, not sounding all that intimidated by the idea. "But what about all the people wearing scary costumes?"

"They're just regular people under those masks."

"Regular people." She's repeating me for her own benefit, trying to convince herself what I'm saying is true.

"Do you have pets?" I ask.

She smiles. "Yes. I have the sweetest little dog."

I put my notebook on the arm of the chair and lean toward her. "Okay, so what if you dressed up your dog as a spider. Have you seen those costumes?"

She shivers. "Yes. They're awful."

"But would it change your dog in any way to you?"

She furrows her brow. "He'd still be my sweet Bentley."

"Exactly. Wearing a costume doesn't change who you are underneath it."

She laughs. "I think he might actually be a cute spider, if there is such a thing."

I smile at her. "Donna, you're making great progress today. Look at you." I gesture to her. "You're laughing and talking about spiders."

She laughs harder. "I am. I can't believe it, but I am."

She's trading one emotion for another, and I suspect the laughter is somewhat out of fear or at least discomfort. Like how tickling someone triggers laughter even if they hate being tickled.

"My friend keeps trying to get me to go to the haunted house the youth center is putting on."

"My friends run the youth center. The kids do a great job every year."

"I don't think I have it in me to go. I mean, picturing Bentley in a costume is one thing, but seeing so many strangers in costume…" She shakes her head.

"I go to the haunted house every year. They have a cute section for little kids. Maybe it would be good for you to go see the kids having fun in that part of the haunted house. I don't think it will be too much for you."

"I don't know." She squeezes her hands together in her lap.

"Look, whether you decide to or not, you've made great progress today. You should be proud of yourself. Consider finding a dress similar to one Greta Garbo wore in *Anna Karenina* for next year. That would give you an entire year to get used to the idea of wearing a costume."

"Maybe. I'll think about it."

I look up at the clock on the wall. "Well, Donna, I'm afraid that's all the time we have for today. I'm really proud of you."

She stands up. "You know, I think I am, too."

I walk her to the door. "See you next week, Donna."

"See ya, Doc." She waves as she exits my office.

Lena Stillwater, my receptionist, looks up at me from her desk. "That's it. You're all finished for the day." She stands up and grabs her purse.

"Big plans tonight?" I ask her. Lena is twenty-seven and not married. She's got a great head on her shoulders, but I'm willing to bet she's got a great social life as well. She strikes me as someone who balances her professional and personal lives well.

"A friend of mine is having a party," she explains as we head for our cars. "Not a big one. Just a few people. We're going to decorate her house for Halloween while watching *Halloween* the movie, the original of course. And, naturally, we'll have some drinks with dinner."

"Sounds fun. Enjoy."

"What about you?" she asks me. "Are you going out with Nolan?"

Nolan Lange is my boyfriend of the past eight months. He moved back to town right before Valentine's Day to work at the local newspaper, and even though we weren't friends growing up, he and I sort of hit it off as if we'd been friends all our lives. The only downside to dating Nolan is his brother, Detective Andrew Lange. Drew sort of despises me. He accused me of murdering a guy I was supposed to have a first date with last Valentine's Day. Nolan is the one who jumped in and helped me prove my innocence by finding the real murderer. To say Nolan and Drew's relationship is strained is a gross understatement. But these days, they just try to avoid each other.

"Nolan and I are going to the haunted house at the youth center. I promised Autumn and Aaron that I'd come support the kids and all the hard work they're doing."

"Well, that should be fun. I love a good haunted house."

"You should check it out. They have it every Thursday through Sunday until the end of the month. All the entry fees are going to programs at the youth center, so it's for a great cause." Autumn and Aaron do so much for the kids in this town. I'm always happy to support their fundraisers like this one.

"I will. I'll see if some of my friends I'll be hanging out with tonight want to go."

I squeeze her arm. "You're the best, Lena. Thanks."

"Sure thing. See you tomorrow morning." She gets in her car, and I open the door of my Altima.

Just as I'm clicking my seat belt, my phone rings through the car's Bluetooth. I answer the call with a smile, knowing it's Nolan without even glancing at the caller ID. "Hi, you."

"How's my favorite psychologist?" he asks.

"I wasn't aware you were seeing one," I tease.

"Only in my free time and on a personal basis."

I smile. "Are we still on for the haunted house tonight?"

"Yup. Pick you up at seven."

"See you then."

I end the call and start counting the minutes until seven.

The crowd waiting to get inside the haunted house is insane. I've never seen the line this long. Autumn, Aaron, and the kids at the youth center must have outdone themselves this year. Everyone exiting the building is either laughing or looking like they just had their lives flash before their eyes. It always amazes me how people react to being scared. Some love it. Others hate it. But even the people who seem a bit traumatized are remarking about how amazing the setup was.

Autumn is taking tickets at the door in a full-on Raggedy Anne costume.

"You look amazing," I tell her, glancing down at my own costume, which is the female version of the Mad Hatter.

Autumn walks around the booth to hug me. "So do you." She turns to Nolan. "What are you supposed to be?"

Nolan is wearing a suit and fake glasses. "I'm Clark Kent."

Autumn narrows her eyes at him. "You could have dressed up as Superman, but you chose to be Clark Kent instead?"

"He's an award-winning reporter," Nolan says as if that somehow makes Clark Kent superior to Superman.

"Wow." Autumn shakes her head. "I don't know how to respond to that, so you two have fun in there."

"I don't get it," Nolan says to me. "What's wrong with my costume?"

I loop my arm through his as we walk inside. "Nothing at all. You're the best Clark Kent I've ever seen." I give him a quick kiss. He does look amazing in that suit, and if he needs to wear glasses one day, they really suit his facial structure.

I recognize one of the boys from the youth center, Kevin Richman. He's eighteen, but he's been coming to the youth center since he was about twelve. I feel like I've watched him grow up. He's dressed in all black and is wielding a bloody knife, but he breaks character and waves to me.

"Hey, Doc." Like many people in town, he prefers to call me Doc instead of Sydney. For him, I suspect it's a respect thing since he doesn't feel comfortable calling me by my first name even if he is technically an adult now.

"Hi, Kevin. You remember Nolan, right?" I ask.

"Yeah, good to see you both."

Someone screams from farther inside the haunted house.

Kevin waves a hand. "That's been happening all night. People have been really spooked by the insane asylum room. It's where I've been stationed for most of the night. It's my break, though."

"We're looking forward to seeing it then," Nolan says, placing his hand on my lower back and nudging me to continue through the haunted house.

Another scream makes me pick up the pace. I'm used to hearing both screams and laughter in this place. People tend to scream first and then laugh when they remember nothing here will actually harm them. But the screams get worse.

Nolan and I exchange a glance and take off down the hallway, ignoring the arms reaching out at us in the darkness. When we reach the asylum, I see someone facedown on the floor.

A woman is standing over the body. "That's real blood. I can smell it." She's covering her nose.

I bend down and touch the body. It's a woman in a dress from the 1930s. If I didn't know better, I'd say she kind of looks like Greta Garbo. But it can't be. I roll her onto her side, and that's when I see the handle of the knife sticking out of the woman's chest.

"It's Donna Barrett," I say, turning away from her and wrapping my arms around Nolan. "She's one of my patients." And she's very much dead.

Chapter Two

Nolan wraps his arm around me as we stand off to the side and watch the coroner zip Donna Barrett's body into a bag. Detective Lange is speaking with the woman who discovered Donna. I overheard her say her name was Olivia Turnbull.

"You're shaking," Nolan says to me. "Are you cold?"

"No. I can't get over the fact that she's dead. I think it's partially my fault she came here tonight."

Nolan presses a finger to his lips and glances in his brother's direction. Detective Lange is busy taking Olivia's statement and not paying attention to us. "Not here. Let's go back to your place and talk."

I nod because I'm sure Detective Lange would love to have a reason to haul me into the station.

After saying goodbye to Autumn and Aaron, who look completely shocked and terrified that someone was murdered in their youth center, Nolan drives me home.

"Think they'll be okay?" I ask him.

"It's awful, but considering they were both working outside, there's no way either will be a suspect. Too many people saw them."

He's right. I take comfort in knowing that Detective Lange won't be able to accuse them of having anything to do with Donna's murder.

"Why did you say it was your fault she went to the haunted house?" Nolan asks as he pulls onto my street.

"I had a session with her this afternoon. She's afraid of Halloween and many things associated with the holiday. I was encouraging her to try to see the fun in the holiday. She actually made great progress. We talked about old movies she liked, and I suggested she consider finding a Greta Garbo costume for next year."

He parks in my driveway and cuts the engine. "Next year? Wait. That would mean she somehow managed to throw a costume together in a matter of hours."

"I know. I can't figure out how that happened, or how she came to be able to attend the haunted house at all. She said one of her friends had mentioned it to her, but that's a big leap to take in such a short amount of time given Donna's fears. It doesn't make sense."

"Do you think she came with that friend?"

I get out of the car and walk up to the front door. "I don't know. She never told me the friend's name either." I unlock the door and walk into the house, which used to belong to my grandmother. "Would you like some coffee or tea to warm up?" It's chilly this evening, and the murder seems to have made everything about tonight seem even colder.

"I'll get it." He walks into the kitchen and starts brewing a pot of coffee. He's made himself at home here over the past eight months. I think it has a lot to do with hating his own tiny apartment, but I hope he's as comfortable around me as I am around him.

I sit down at the center island and remove the hat from my head. I'm still in costume, but I don't have the energy to get changed out of it. Nolan removes his fake glasses, putting them in the pocket of his dress shirt after taking off the suit jacket and placing it on the back of one of the chairs at the kitchen table.

"Why don't you go take a nice hot shower while I get the coffee ready?" he suggests.

"I would if I had the strength or will to get up off this stool."

He walks over and kisses the top of my head. "Want me to walk you to the bathroom?"

I'm about to say no when I realize I will feel better after showering and getting into pajamas. "Okay."

He offers me his hand to help me off the stool, and then he walks me to my room where I grab a change of clothes. "Are you hungry?" he asks me.

"A little."

"I'll order us some wanton soup and egg rolls," he says.

"It's like you can read my mind." I smile at him as I walk into the bathroom and close the door. I take a long shower, but it does nothing to ease my tension. My shoulders still feel like they're up by my ears. I have no idea how things got so out of control. Donna shouldn't have been at that haunted house. No one would have suspected she would be, so there's no way this was a premeditated murder. Was someone else the intended target, and Donna simply was in the wrong place at the wrong time? It was dark in the asylum room. You could only see when the electric shock therapy machine was switched on. Otherwise, the room was in complete darkness. It's possible the killer meant to stab someone else entirely.

The irony of the situation isn't lost on me. Donna was terrified of Halloween and everything associated with it, and when she tried to confront her fears—possibly because I put the idea in her head—she wound up getting murdered.

"Sydney?" Nolan calls through the bathroom door. "Are you okay? It sounds like you're crying in there."

I look into the mirror above the sink. I don't even remember drying off or getting into my pajamas. Nolan's right, too. Tears are streaming down my face. I use my towel to dab my cheeks. Then I hang the towel on the hook on the back of the door and exit the bathroom.

Nolan takes one look at me and cocks his head. "That was supposed to make you feel better, not worse."

"Sorry."

"Don't apologize." He wraps me in a hug.

"I don't know what convinced her to go to the haunted house, but I can't help thinking she never would have if we didn't have our session today."

He walks me back to the kitchen, his arm around me. "You can't blame yourself for helping her."

"It's just not fair." I sit down at the kitchen table, where Nolan has the soup in two bowls for us and the egg rolls on plates. I'm not even sure I can eat anymore.

He picks up my spoon and hands it to me. "Eat. You need to."

I take a spoonful of soup to appease him. "I should call Autumn and make sure she's okay. Leslie, the woman that helps manage the youth center, took some vacation time, so Autumn is shorthanded as it is."

"She has Aaron, just like you have me. You need time to process right now. Stop worrying about everyone else."

"But your brother—"

"Is a jerk. I'm well aware. We'll deal with him in the morning."

"Has your boss called?" I ask. Being that Nolan was on the scene, his boss will want him to cover the story.

"Yeah, he called while you were in the shower. I'll be interviewing people tomorrow, and I have to write up an article to run immediately as well. I already started it."

How long was my shower?

"Don't let me keep you from your work," I tell him.

"I'll handle it. The article is due in an hour, and it's already half written. Eat." He motions to my food before biting into his egg roll.

The good news is since Nolan is covering the story, he'll be talking to everyone who might be connected to the murder. That will allow me to tag along and get some answers myself. I'm not about to sit back and hope Detective Drew Lange solves this on his own.

After dinner, Nolan goes to the living room to finish writing his article on my laptop, and I head to bed, knowing full well I'll find Nolan asleep on my couch in the morning.

My Saturday morning sessions go smoothly, and before I know it, I'm ready to clock out for the day, so to speak. Then my phone rings. At first, I think it has to be Detective Drew Lange wanting to question me about Donna Barrett because he found out she was a client of mine. I'm relieved and happy to see Nolan's picture on my phone screen.

"Hey, you were gone before I woke up," I say.

"Yeah, I wanted to get to the office early. How did you sleep?"

"Better than I thought I would." I must have been so emotionally exhausted that I passed out. I don't even remember having a single dream.

"Are you almost finished with clients for the day?" he asks, knowing I only work a half day on Saturdays.

"I finished about five minutes ago. Where are you off to?" I stand up from my desk and grab my purse and car keys.

"Is that your way of asking where you can meet me to get some information on the case?" he asks.

"You know me so well."

"That I do. I figured I should start with getting Autumn's and Aaron's thoughts since it happened at their youth center."

Another reporter might do so only for that reason, but I know Nolan wants to talk to them so he can hopefully assure the public that the youth center and its employees and kids had nothing to do with the murder. He's looking out for our friends.

"Great idea. I'll meet you there."

"Can't wait. I think I forgot what you look like."

I walk to my car, waving to Lena on the way out of the office. "Really? After a few hours, you've already forgotten what I look like? That doesn't sound like very good reporter skills to me. Aren't you supposed to have a good memory?" The parking lot is empty except for Lena's car. I start mine, switching my call to the car's Bluetooth, and pull out onto the road.

"Oh, wait." I hear him snap his fingers on the other end. "Sydney, brown hair, blue eyes. Yeah, it's coming back to me now."

"Lucky for you or I would have made plans with someone else for tonight."

"Ouch. You'd date someone else that quickly? And here I thought you loved me."

I turn into the parking lot of the youth center and see Nolan standing outside his car, his phone to his ear. I cut the engine and get out.

"And now you hung up on me," Nolan says, walking over to me.

"Sorry, I got distracted by this incredibly handsome man in the parking lot." I step toward him and kiss him hello. "Thanks for waiting for me."

"I'm not just a pretty face," he jokes. "I'm smart, too. Besides, I've heard how quickly you'd replace me."

I laugh. "Come on. You're clearly fishing for compliments today."

He holds his thumb and index finger about a quarter of an inch apart. "Only a little."

"Fine. You're incredibly handsome, smart, and I love you. Better?" I ask.

"Much." He smiles and offers me his arm before we walk into the youth center.

As soon as we step inside, my smile falters. Detective Lange is talking to Autumn and Aaron. Nolan and I exchange worried looks before we interrupt their conversation.

"What's going on, Detective?" I ask him as I give Autumn a hug.

"Syd, Detective Lange wants to talk to some of the kids, but they're just kids, which means their parents or guardians have to be contacted. I'm not sure why he needs to question them anyway. They're kids, not killers." Autumn practically spits the last sentence at him.

"Mrs. Young, I've already told you this is standard procedure. I need to talk to everyone who was in that room or who had access to it last night."

Autumn throws out her arm. "You might as well talk to half the town. Do you have any idea how many people were here last night?" She scoffs.

"I don't suppose you took names," he says.

"It's a haunted house, not a classroom. We didn't take attendance." Autumn's hatred for Andrew Lange is well-known. She doesn't try to mask it at all.

"It's okay, Autumn; it's Detective Lange's job to contact all the parents and guardians of the kids he wants to speak with," I say.

Detective Lange's jaw clenches. "Always a pleasure to see you, Sydney."

"It's Doctor Warner to you," I say.

Detective Lange turns back to Aaron, who I'm assuming is slightly more cooperative than Autumn or me. "I need a list of all the kids who were working the haunted house last night."

Aaron nods. He squeezes Autumn's hand before disappearing into their shared office.

I pull Autumn toward the game room. "I'm guessing you closed the place today," I say, looking around.

"Detective Lange made us. Until the police are finished with their investigation, I can't let the kids come here. He has no idea how much some of these kids need this place. All he's thinking about is himself."

And Donna Barrett. "He does have a murder to solve. Can't you have the kids meet you at a different site until this is over?" I suggest.

She looks up for a moment, and I know she's trying to figure out how to make that work. "The library has a conference room upstairs. I wonder if they'll let me book it for the week. I could have the kids meet me there. It won't be the same, but it's better than them having nowhere to go."

"You should call the library and find out."

She nods. "I'll go do that. Thanks, Syd." She walks to the office, and I go back to Nolan, who is talking to Drew.

"I'm covering the case for the paper, Drew. There's nothing you can do about it," Nolan says.

"Just stay out of my way, or I will arrest you for obstruction."

"Hey," I say, stepping between them. "Don't you think it's about time you two ended this little family feud? I mean you're grown men."

"I'm not about to take advice from you," Detective Lange says.

"No, who would take advice from a psychologist? That would be completely absurd," I say, my words dripping with sarcasm. "I can totally see your point."

"Ha-ha." Detective Lange crosses his arms. "Where's Aaron with that list already?"

The door behind Detective Lange opens, and Kevin Richman walks in. I rush over to him.

"Kevin, you shouldn't be here," I say. "You need to leave."

Detective Lange marches up to us. "Did you work the haunted house last night?"

Kevin nods.

Detective Lange looks him up and down. "How old are you?"

Before I can try to tell Kevin he shouldn't answer that question, he blurts out, "Eighteen."

I close my eyes and sigh.

"Great. You're a legal adult. I have a few questions to ask you."

Kevin might be a legal adult, but he looks like a scared toddler right now, and I'm not sure how to help him.

Chapter Three

I'm not about to let Detective Lange bring poor Kevin to the station in handcuffs, and I know how quick Andrew Lange is to jump to conclusions. I have firsthand experience being on the receiving end of his accusations.

"You'll need to come with me," Detective Lange tells him.

"Come where? What's going on?" Kevin looks to Autumn and then me.

There's only one way I can think of to get Kevin out of this. "Detective, you can talk to Kevin right here with me present."

Detective Lange's head whips in my direction. "You're not his legal guardian, and he's an adult."

"I'm Kevin's psychologist. I have every right to be here." I eye Kevin, trying to mentally convey that he needs to play along. He doesn't have parents to come to his defense, and I'm positive he can't afford a lawyer. I'm his best option.

"Really?" Detective Lange asks with the quirk of an eyebrow. "See, that I didn't know, but I do know you were Donna Barrett's therapist. I found her appointment with you on the calendar in her phone."

"That's right. I was."

"I'm going to need to talk to you about your session with her yesterday."

"What Donna and I discussed privately is confidential," I say. Of course, I did tell Nolan, which I shouldn't have. But Donna is dead, and I'm not sure she'd mind me telling Nolan about her progress during our session.

"If you have information that can help me solve her murder—"

"I don't think I do. I didn't know she was going to the haunted house."

Nolan steps toward his brother. "Come on, Drew. You know this is hard on Syd. Why do you have to always play detective?"

"I'm not playing anything. I am a detective. Just like you're a reporter. Like you said, you're covering this story." He steps toward Nolan, eyeing him up and down. "You might be fooling her, but you don't fool me. You're using her for information and playing it off as being the concerned boyfriend."

Nolan pulls his arm back to punch Drew, but I grab him.

"Don't." We both know Drew would put his brother in jail for assaulting him. Once Nolan lowers his arm, lacing his fingers through mine, probably to keep from being tempted to punch his brother, I turn to Drew. "Nolan is nothing like you, Detective. He actually has a heart." I motion to Kevin. "He might be eighteen, but he doesn't have parents to support him right now. I'm going to have to insist I'm present when you talk to him."

Kevin nods. "I want Doc Warner with me."

Detective Lange rubs his forehead, just over his eyebrows, with his thumb and index finger. "Fine." He looks at Autumn. "Do you have a room we could use for this conversation?"

I admit I'm surprised he not only gave in about me being present, but he's allowing us to do it here instead of down at the station. Is it possible there is a heart buried somewhere deep inside him?

"You can use the game room. No one is in there." Autumn motions to it. "The door is unlocked."

I give her arm a squeeze, hopefully conveying I'll do my best to take care of Kevin.

Detective Lange opens the door and ushers Kevin and me inside, but he puts up a hand to stop Nolan. "No press," he says.

"You're kidding, right?" Nolan asks.

"Not even a little bit." Detective Lange closes the door in Nolan's face.

"Was that really necessary?" I ask him.

Detective Lange turns to me. "Necessary? No. Fun? Very much so." He smirks.

Kevin is standing by the pool table, running his fingers over the green felt. I walk over to him and place my hand on his shoulder for reassurance.

Detective Lange removes a small notepad and pen from his shirt pocket under his jacket. "State your full name."

I nudge Kevin to get his attention.

"Oh, um, Kevin Richman."

"Kevin, you worked the haunted house last night?"

"Yes."

"What was your role in the haunted house?"

"I was supposed to pop out of the shadows with my knife and scare people."

"Where is that knife?" Detective Lange asks, looking up from his notepad.

"It's rubber. I have it at my place."

"And where is your place? I'm told you have no legal guardians."

Kevin swallows hard, and I squeeze his shoulder.

"It's okay, Kevin."

"My parents were killed in a car accident a few years ago. I was with a foster family until I turned eighteen. Then I moved into a one-bedroom apartment above the laundromat on First Street."

"Did you see the victim at any point last night?"

"Yeah. She was with another woman."

"The friend she mentioned," I say.

"What?" Detective Lange narrows his eyes at me. "You were aware of this as well?"

"No. I was trying to figure out what brought Donna to the haunted house in the first place. She was afraid of costumes and Halloween in general, but she mentioned…" I know Donna is dead and telling Detective Lange this might help solve her murder, but it feels wrong to disclose what she told me during our session.

"Look, Sydney, I can get a court order for you to release your notes to me. Do I really need to do that?"

Actually, that would make me feel a lot better. "I'd appreciate it. Thanks."

"That wasn't an offer," he practically growls.

"All the same, let's do that."

Detective Lange is fuming. His face is bright red, and I'm not sure he's breathing. He turns back to Kevin. "Who was the woman Donna Barrett was with?"

"I don't know." He shrugs.

"What did she look like?" Drew's tone is indicating he's lost all patience with both of us.

"It's hard to say. She was in costume."

Detective Lange points his finger in Kevin's face. "Listen, I've had enough games. You can either answer my questions, or I'll throw you in a holding cell until you're ready to cooperate."

"Hey!" I yell, and at the rise in my voice, Nolan forces his way into the room.

"What's going on?" he asks, his gaze immediately going to me.

"Detective, Kevin is cooperating. It was dark inside the haunted house. You could barely see yourself, let alone anyone else. And everyone was in costume. You can't possibly expect him or me to be able to identify anyone we saw there."

"He remembered seeing the victim and that she wasn't alone," Detective Lange says.

Nolan comes to stand beside me, placing his hand on my back. "You have the victim's phone. If she had plans to attend the haunted house with a friend, I'm sure there's some mention of it in a text, or there's a recent phone call you could trace back to someone."

Detective Lange zeros in on Nolan. "I don't need to be told how to do my job, thank you."

"You needed to be told people were in costume at a haunted house," I say.

"That's not typical," Detective Lange says. "Halloween is next week. Why was everyone dressed up?"

He's not wrong about that. But it's a requirement the youth center has every year because there's a costume contest. "Every guest gets their picture taken as they leave the haunted house.

Those pictures are then displayed on the youth center's website. People donate fifty cents for every vote they make, and the winner is revealed on Halloween night," I explain. "Autumn and Aaron have been holding the contest for the past three years."

Kevin bobs his head in agreement.

Detective Lange scribbles in his notepad. "What costume was the woman with Donna Barrett wearing?" he asks.

I turn to Kevin since I can't help him with this question.

"I'm not sure. I think maybe she was a flapper from the 1920s. I just watched a movie set in the twenties, and she looked like the women in that. She was wearing a blonde wig and one of those flapper-style dresses. She stood out because her entire outfit was white. She practically glowed in the dark."

"I didn't see anyone like that when I got here," Detective Lange says.

"Neither did I, and I got to the body right after all the screaming started."

"She means after Olivia Turnbull discovered Donna's body," Nolan says.

Would Donna's friend drag her to the haunted house, kill her, and run before the police showed up? I know that's what Detective Lange is thinking happened, but right now there's zero motive. I guess I should be happy he's not blaming Kevin, Nolan, or me, but I'm not as quick to jump to conclusions as he is.

Detective Lange looks to me. "I need to see your notes on your sessions with Donna."

I was just thinking I need to go over them as well. "I'll be happy to supply you with copies as soon as you get that court order, Detective."

"The woman is dead, Sydney."

"It's Doctor Warner, thank you, and feel free to contact me when you have the necessary documents. I'm going to walk Kevin out now." I motion for Kevin to go first.

"I don't believe I dismissed anyone," Detective Lange says. "Despite what you may think, this isn't your investigation, Sydney." I know he's purposely calling me by my first name to get a rise out of me.

"You have no evidence to hold either of us, so I think we're finished here." I smile and turn around, nudging Kevin through the door.

Autumn hurries over to us. "Kevin, are you all right?"

"Yeah, Doc handled it," he says.

Autumn nods a silent thank you to me.

Detective Lange walks out of the game room and past us all without saying a word.

"No offense, Nolan, but your brother is a real jerk," Autumn says.

"No offense taken. I call him a lot worse."

"Where's Aaron?" I ask.

Autumn hitches a thumb over her shoulder. "In the office calling everyone's parents to give them the heads-up that Detective Lange is going to want to speak to their children."

"If you want me there, just call me," I tell her.

"I think I'm going to wait for the bus," Kevin says. "I want to go home." Kevin can't afford a car, so he takes the bus everywhere.

"I'll drive you," Autumn says. "Let me grab my car keys." She disappears inside her office.

"I'm going to head back to my office and go through my notes," I tell Nolan.

"Do you want help?"

It's an ethical issue. I've already told him more than I feel comfortable with. "I think I should go through them alone."

He nods. "I get it, but I can come with you to your office and look through Donna's social media profiles. You know, do a little research of my own."

"Okay, sounds like a plan."

After saying goodbye to Autumn and Kevin, Nolan and I drive to my office. He uses the couch to conduct his research, while I take my desk.

Donna's notebook is pretty full since she's been coming to see me for about a year and a half now. Her main reason for coming to me was to help her deal with her phobias, which don't end with Halloween. She was afraid of elevators, which she believed would cause her to plummet to her death, kind of like those thrill rides many amusement parks created. And like a lot of people, Donna had a fear of being alone. Until I met Nolan, I had that same fear.

My luck in the love department has never been good, which is why I sometimes worry Nolan is too good to be true. Not that Nolan doesn't have flaws. Everyone does. But Nolan's biggest flaw is that he was born Drew Lange's brother, and that's not something he had any control over, so I can't really hold it against him.

I find an interesting passage in my notes from a month ago that draws my attention.

Donna talks about her boyfriend, who she refuses to name, as if he's afraid of commitment. They've been together for six months, and she says he dismissed the idea of moving in together. She told me she believes he's old-fashioned and wants to get married first, so she started dropping hints that she wants him to propose. None of her hints have worked, increasing her fear that she'll wind up old and alone one day.

"She had a boyfriend," I say. "She hasn't talked about him in nearly a month. I sort of forgot he existed. She never told me his name, but she was secretive when it came to naming people in her life."

"I'll check for pictures she might have posted with the same man," Nolan says.

I go back to my notes, looking for any other mention of this boyfriend. I asked her about him three weeks ago, but she dismissed the topic completely, bringing up an issue she was having at work instead. Donna worked in medical billing and coding, which was a remote job, but her boss wanted her to start coming in to the office a few days a week. Donna had friends and a boyfriend, but she told me she needs complete silence to work. She was afraid she wouldn't be able to do her job from anywhere but the comfort of her home.

"I found someone," Nolan says, and I look up from my notes. "Donna tagged a guy named Pierce Crawford in several photos three months ago at a beach party they attended."

"Any chance your investigative skills landed an address for Pierce Crawford as well?"

"Working on that now," he says.

Something Donna said to me in one of our sessions comes back to me. *Cupid really pierced my heart with his arrow this time.* She was cleverly telling me the man's name was Pierce. I wonder if she ever did that again. Was she trying to let me in more in her own roundabout way?

"Okay, no address, but his social media profiles say he works at Arrow Glass Company. They repair windshields, windows, or anything glass really."

Donna's words ring through my head again. She told me "Pierce" and "arrow." She was given me insights into her personal life. I just didn't know it at the time. What else did she tell me that I didn't pick up on? I close the notebook, determined to bring it home with me so I can study it in closer detail later.

"Let's go pay a visit a to Pierce Crawford. I want to find out why Donna stopped talking about him."

"Do you think they broke up?" Nolan asks, standing up from the couch.

"All I know is, Donna was on edge more than usual, and I have a feeling Halloween was actually the least of her concerns."

Chapter Four

Nolan and I stop at a pizza place for lunch before we go to Arrow Glass Company. The pizza place is on the same road, and since it's lunchtime, I'm not really expecting Pierce Crawford to be around right now anyway.

"This is good pizza," Nolan says.

I bob my head since my mouth is full. After swallowing and washing it down with some ginger ale, I say, "I wonder if Pierce comes in here a lot."

"We could ask the waitress. She might know him." He raises his hand in the air to get her attention, and she comes around the counter to our table.

"Can I get you something else?" she asks.

"No, we're fine. We were wondering if you know Pierce Crawford. He works up the street at Arrow Glass Company."

"Mr. Crawford usually orders delivery. He doesn't come in here to eat. He has a standing Friday order each week."

"Do you happen to deliver the food?" I ask.

"No, that's Bucky."

"Bucky?" I ask.

The waitress looks over her shoulder and yells, "Bucky, get out here." When she turns back to us, she says, "He's in the back. He assembles to-go boxes when he's not out making deliveries."

A young guy, probably no older than nineteen or twenty, comes out of the kitchen and looks around. The waitress waves him over to our table.

The bell over the door chimes, and the waitress says, "Excuse me," before rushing back to the counter to help them.

Bucky shoves his hands into his pants pockets. "Um, can I help you with something? Do you need a to-go box?"

"Are you Bucky?" I ask.

"Yeah. I mean, my real name is Terrance Buckman, but every-one calls me Bucky."

"We hear you deliver to Pierce Crawford at Arrow Glass Com-pany every Friday."

He smiles. "Yeah, he's a good tipper."

"Is he a nice guy?" Nolan asks.

Bucky bobs his shoulders, his hands still in his pockets. "I guess so. I mean we don't talk or anything. He orders the same thing every week, so I don't even need to tell him how much he owes. I just hand him the pizza, and he gives me a twenty and tells me to keep the change. I thank him, and that's all the talking we do."

"Do you ever see a woman with him?" I ask, curious if Donna ever met him for lunch on a Friday.

"You mean like a customer or a girlfriend?"

"A girlfriend," I say.

"Not sure. There was this woman with him one time, but they were arguing. I guess it could have been a fight between two people who were dating. I don't know, though."

"Did you hear what they were arguing about?" I ask.

He shakes his head. "I only know the woman looked angry, and Mr. Crawford seemed in a hurry to take his pizza and go eat. I didn't ask questions because it was none of my business."

No, it wouldn't be. He's a pizza delivery guy. "Thanks for your help," I say.

"Not sure I did anything, but you're welcome all the same." He walks away.

"You ready to hit the road?" Nolan asks, wiping his hands on a napkin.

I take the last sip of my ginger ale and stand up. "Let's do it." Since we paid at the counter ahead of time, we leave a tip on the table and wave to the waitress as we leave.

Arrow Glass Company is a building with an attached garage. The garage appears to only be able to house one car at a time, but since they fix all kinds of glass here, I suppose that's sufficient. The building itself is like a big showroom with different windows, glass tables, and even glass figurines on display. In the back is a counter with a man sitting on a stool. Nolan and I walk up to him.

"Pierce Crawford?" Nolan asks.

The man looks up from the magazine he's reading. "That's me. What can I do for you?" He closes the magazine and puts it on the counter.

Nolan holds up his reporter's ID badge. I'm Nolan Lange, a reporter with the *Swan Creek Gazette*. We'd like to talk to you about Donna Barrett."

Pierce stands up and lowers his head. "I heard what happened to her."

Heard? The way he says it is as if they aren't still dating. "Mr. Crawford, we were under the impression you and Donna were romantically involved," I say.

"We were. We broke up a few weeks ago."

"Oh, I see. When did you see her last?"

"Um, about two weeks ago. She came here to pick up some of her stuff she had left at my apartment."

Bucky didn't mention the woman having anything with her or carrying a box of any nature, but we never asked about that either.

"Was it a bad breakup?" Nolan asks.

"Why does it matter? I haven't seen or spoken to her in two weeks. Why are you asking me questions?"

"We aren't sure who Donna was with the night she was murdered," I say. "We know it was a woman, though. We were hoping you might be able to help us identify her." I figure it's best if he doesn't think we suspect him of killing Donna. He'll be more willing to talk to us if he thinks we just need him to point us in a direction.

"Oh. To be honest, I was shocked when I heard it happened at a haunted house. Donna hates—hated that sort of thing."

"Can you think of anyone with a strong enough personality to talk her into it?" I ask. "Maybe a friend who was usually encouraging Donna to get out more or try new things?"

"Um, she talked to this woman named Cara a lot."

"You don't happen to know Cara's last name, do you?" Nolan asks.

Pierce shakes his head. "No. I met her a few times at parties, though. She was very outgoing. Pretty. She was kind of Donna's opposite in a lot of ways."

"How so?" I ask.

"I remember Cara made a comment at this beach party we all went to. She said she'd never get married and settle down. She thought life was too short for that sort of thing."

"And Donna felt differently about the subject?" I ask, playing dumb.

Pierce's eyes widen, and he sighs. "It's the reason we split up. She became obsessed with marriage. I put up with it for a while, thinking she'd get over it. I mean, we'd only been dating for like three months when she first mentioned it. But she wouldn't let it go. In fact, it got worse. I couldn't take it anymore. I told her she was moving too fast, and I needed time apart."

"How did she react to that?" Nolan asks.

"Not well. She lashed out at me. Told me I'd wasted her time, and at our age that was criminal." He scoffs. "I'm thirty-four. She was only thirty. I don't see the big rush. Maybe her biological clock was ticking or whatever." He waves a hand in the air.

"You don't seem all that upset over the breakup or Donna's death," Nolan says, and I know the comment is going to make Pierce go on the defensive again.

"Well, can you blame him?" I say, jumping in before Pierce can react. "It sounds like he tried to reason with her, but she wouldn't let it go." I look at Pierce. "Was that her personality? To push and push like that?"

"Not really. She had disagreements with a lot of people, though. I think that's why she liked to work from home. I think she knew she lacked certain people skills."

"Who did she have disagreements with?" I ask.

"Well, there was her neighbor. Donna called the cops on her numerous times, complaining about noise violations after ten o'clock." Pierce shakes his head. "I swear, sometimes she acted like she was eighty years old. I mean, yeah, the neighbor set off fireworks at ten thirty at night, but it was the Fourth of July after all. It's kind of to be expected. But one hit Donna's house, and she swore the woman did it on purpose."

"Did it damage the house?" Nolan asks.

"Donna claimed it did, but I saw it. It was the tiniest little singe mark. Donna made a big deal out of it, though. She even threatened to sue."

Donna never mentioned this to me in our sessions. Why would she come to see me every week if she wasn't going to be honest with me about what was going on in her life?

"The neighbor threw a few parties, too. Donna called the cops every time people were still over in the woman's backyard after ten o'clock."

I suppose this neighbor isn't too upset Donna's gone. Or did she finally retaliate and kill Donna so she couldn't meddle in her life anymore? The more I learn about Donna, the less I feel like I knew her. It's almost as if she just wanted to pay someone to listen to her talk. I never had a chance to help her because she was lying to me. Or was she paranoid? What if she thought she was always being watched, and she thought she couldn't come out and tell me what was really going on in her life? Was someone threatening her? Watching her every move? Did she want to open up to me but couldn't because she feared it would cost her her life?

That would explain the way she managed to sneak Pierce's name into our session and the clue about where he worked. I need to dissect every session we had together in case there are more clues, because right now, the only one I've found leads to this man right here. What if she was afraid of him, and she purposely pushed the marriage issue to get him to leave her? It could have all been an act to get free from him.

This case is making me feel like I need to lie down on a couch and talk to a therapist.

"This is my card," Nolan says, drawing me back to the conversation. "If you think of anything else that might be helpful, please call me."

"Should I expect the police to come by?" Pierce asks.

I study his body language to see if that thought frightens him. He remains completely stoic, though.

"It's possible," Nolan says. "If and when you meet Detective Lange, just know we're not brother's by choice."

"The detective on the case is your brother?" Pierce asks.

"Only by blood. I don't actually consider him family." Nolan turns around and reaches for my hand. I take one last look at Pierce before letting Nolan lead me out of the store.

"Where did you go back there?" he asks once we're inside the car.

"Sorry for zoning out, but my mind started racing with possibilities. Donna kept a lot from me."

"Why would she do that? You wouldn't be able to help her."

"Exactly. So did she not tell me what was really going on with her because she was afraid to?"

"Do you think she knew someone had it in for her?" he asks.

"All I know is she never mentioned the people in her life by name, and there has to be a reason why."

"That would imply she knew her killer. This wasn't random by any means."

I never thought it was, but I guess as a reporter, he has to remain neutral and consider all the possibilities. "No. This definitely wasn't random. This person knew Donna would be at the haunted house last night. They went there with the intention to kill her."

"If only we had access to her phone the way Drew does."

"We know he's interviewing the people who worked at the haunted house first. Why? Why not look into Donna's phone to see who she was going to the haunted house with?"

"Because my brother is an idiot."

"Or did he tell us he was starting with the kids who worked the haunted house to throw us off his trail?" I ask.

"You think he was purposely feeding us bad information?"

"Think about it." I twist in the passenger seat so I'm facing him. "He knew if he went to Autumn and Aaron for a list of kids who worked at the haunted house, Autumn would call me immediately to tell me about it."

"And then we jumped in to help Kevin right in front of him."

I snap my fingers. "That's why he didn't insist on bringing Kevin down to the police station for questioning. He never thought it was him!" I knew that was completely out of character for Detective Lange. It was staged. He set us up.

"I can't believe he played us," Nolan says. "Just when I think I can't hate the man any more than I already do…"

I reach for his leg and squeeze it. I don't like Drew, but I hate that Nolan's relationship with his brother is so awful. Nolan deserves so much better. The other night I overheard him on the phone with his parents in Florida, and he lied and told them he and Drew were getting along great. He's covering for Drew, not for Drew's sake but for his parents'. Poor Nolan.

"I'm all right." He places his hand on top of mine.

"I have a plan," I say.

"Good. It will help get my mind off the fact that I really want to punch Drew in the face."

"Actually, I'm not sure it will since my plan is to follow your brother to figure out what lead he's really pursuing."

"You want to stalk a police detective?" he asks.

It wouldn't be the first time I did it. But this time, I have to make sure Detective Lange doesn't catch me in the act.

Chapter Five

"How do we find him?" I ask Nolan. It's not like we can call his wife, although, she's actually nice. I'm not sure how Annabelle wound up with a man like Drew.

"I can ask around with the other reporters at the paper and see if any have crossed paths with him today." Nolan gets on the phone to do just that, so I call Autumn.

"Hey, Syd. Thanks again for your help with Kevin this morning."

"Don't mention it. I was happy to help him out. I'm calling because Nolan and I are wondering if any of the kids at the youth center were questioned by Detective Lange yet today."

"Other than Kevin, I'm not sure. Aaron called all their parents to let them know the police want to talk to everyone who worked at the haunted house, but we haven't heard back from anyone saying they were questioned. Why?"

"Because I don't think Detective Lange is looking into your kids. I think he said that because he wanted to throw Nolan and me off his scent."

"Why would he keep his investigation from you? That's just petty."

"I don't know. Maybe because I beat him to the punch when it came to solving two cases already."

"Yeah, but you haven't gotten involved in one of his cases since the Fourth of July." She pauses. "Oh, but he'd assume you'd get involved in this one because it happened at my youth center and involved one of your clients. Okay, I'm following now. I clearly need more caffeine today. My brain is a little slow."

"No worries. I need to figure out who Drew might have gone to question."

"If I were Drew, and that's the scariest what-if scenario I've ever mentioned in my life, I would find out who Donna came to the haunted house with."

"You didn't see the woman?" I ask. "I'm thinking it was Donna's friend Cara, but I've come to discover Donna kept an awful lot of secrets from me."

"Well, that was stupid of her. Why would she do that?"

"I don't know. I don't think she was a very trusting person. Maybe she was testing me."

"For like a year and a half? That's a lot of money to pay to test out someone's trustworthiness."

"I agree. I wish I could make sense of it, or even share these files with someone else."

"You're going to have to share them with Detective Lange when he gets that court order to force you to hand them over."

"Autumn, you just gave me the idea I needed. Thank you!"

"What idea? What did I do?"

"I've got to go. I'll fill you in later." I hang up, and Nolan furrows his brow at me. He's still on his call but clearly knows I'm up to something. I dial the Swan Creek Police Department. "Yes, I need to speak with Detective Lange. This is Doctor Sydney Warner, and I have some notes he requested on Donna Barrett."

"Detective Lange isn't in the office at the moment," the woman says.

"I see. Well, tell him I'll be at my office until six. He can meet me there. He knows where it is." I hang up.

"What are you doing?" Nolan asks, finished with his own call.

"Why track down Drew when I have exactly what I need to bring him straight to us?"

"You're going to hand over your notes to him?"

"Copies. I'll print them out for him. I still have my original notebook and the files in my computer. But I'm thinking if I tell him what I decoded from Donna's cryptic sessions, maybe he can help me track down this Cara woman and anyone else I might not have picked up on from Donna's conversations."

Nolan holds up a hand. "Let me get this straight. You want to work alongside my brother."

Want is a strong word. More like I need to. "At this point, I don't care if he finds the killer or if I do. I want the person caught and brought to justice."

"Okay, but Syd, if you're thinking that by you sharing information with Drew, he's going to reciprocate and tell you what he knows, you're going to be disappointed. That's not how Drew operates. He doesn't care about anyone but himself."

No. There is someone else he cares about. Annabelle. "We may need to get ourselves invited for dinner at Drew and Annabelle's house," I say.

Nolan leans his head back on the head rest. "Now I'm starting to worry about you. Drew is not going to invite us for dinner. Ever."

"He let us stay the night at his house back in February."

"Because we were supposed to be under police protection. And need I remind you that we escaped, and he got a ton of grief for it? Believe me. He holds grudges. He's not over that."

"But Annabelle likes you. She wants you and Drew to get along. I could see it in her eyes. If she thinks she can bring you two together, even for just one meal, she's going to pounce on the idea."

"How do we even go about doing that?" Nolan asks.

"Call her up. Tell her you've been giving it a lot of thought, and you'd like to make amends with Drew. See what she says." I'm willing to bet a month's pay she invites him over for dinner tomorrow, if not tonight. I motion to his phone.

"Now? You want me to call her right now?"

I nod.

"But if she calls Drew before he gets the message to come to your office, he might suspect this is all a trap."

Hmm, he might be right about that. "Okay, drive to my office. That's where he's meeting us. Once he gets there, you can excuse yourself and call Annabelle. I'll try to keep him occupied if his phone rings while he's looking over the files."

Nolan starts the car. "That could work."

"Thanks for always going along with my crazy plans," I say as he pulls out of the parking lot and onto the road. Even when he first moved back to town, he so easily went along with my ideas.

"The craziest plans usually yield the best results," he says with a smile.

Lena is gone for the day, enjoying her weekend like a normal person, so I unlock the office and let us inside. Detective Lange hasn't shown up yet or tried to call either of us, but I'm sure he'll come. He won't be able to resist getting his hands on my notes. I quickly pull up the file and press print.

"This is going to take a while. I hope there's enough toner in the printer."

"I'd imagine a year and a half would make for a lot of notes."

I'm worried most are worthless. Donna wasn't a typical patient. I'm not sure if she wanted help or only wanted a place to vent. But even if it was just to vent, why wouldn't she talk about her neighbor she was fighting with or her boyfriend? She must not have fully trusted me. And there I was thinking we'd made such great progress in our last session.

I stand at the printer behind Lena's desk, watching the papers come spitting out of the machine.

"You okay?" Nolan asks, coming up behind me.

"Yeah, but I'm wondering why Donna didn't want to use our time together more wisely."

"I'm sure she had a reason, and we'll figure out what it was."

The door to the waiting room opens, and Detective Lange walks in. "I hear you've come to your senses and are actually going to cooperate."

"I want Donna's killer to be caught. If this helps achieve that goal, then so be it. But I think you should know that Donna wasn't the most forthright of my patients."

He crosses his arms. "What is that supposed to mean?"

"I think she wasn't honest with me about everything happening in her life. She withheld a lot of information, which means what you're looking for might not be in these notes."

"I'll be the judge of that." He juts his chin toward the printer. "Are those the notes?"

"Yeah, I hope you like to read because there are a lot of them."

He doesn't look thrilled in the least.

Nolan hitches a thumb toward my office. "I have to check in with my boss. Syd, do you mind if I use your office?"

"Go right ahead," I say, knowing he's going to call Annabelle Lange and try to get us invited for dinner. If it works, I have to hope sharing information with Drew in front of Annabelle will make her encourage him to share information with me in return. If it doesn't, he'll be getting a tail in the form of a psychologist and a journalist.

Nolan walks into my office and closes the door behind him.

I try to play up the ruse by rolling my eyes and saying, "His boss is so secretive about everything. As if there's really anything that big happening in Swan Creek."

"I'd say a murder investigation is pretty big," Detective Lange says.

"Sure, it's not an everyday occurrence, but Nolan's boss acts like the tiniest story is a huge deal."

"I'll admit I'm not at fan of Milton Burke. The man thinks way too highly of himself."

I have to resist the urge to laugh out loud since that's exactly how I'd describe Drew. Pot meet kettle.

"How much longer until that's finished printing?" Detective Lange asks.

I turn back to the printer and pick up the stack of papers. "Do you want to start reading through it while you wait?"

He shakes his head. "No, I'd like to take it with me."

That's fine. We can compare notes later. "Suit yourself." I hand him the first stack. "It will be a little longer. That's only the first year."

His eyes widen at the stack. "Are you always this thorough with your notes?"

"It's sort of my job. People don't just pay me to listen to them talk, you know."

"I've never been to a psychologist, but you can't tell me you actually solve people's problems." He scoffs like it's absurd.

"Well, let's see. Donna was afraid of everything related to Halloween, yet she went to a haunted house. What does that tell you?"

"That you led her to her death."

I narrow my eyes at him. "I didn't suggest she go to the haunted house. I suggested she dress up like Greta Garbo, which she did."

"Is that what her costume was? I couldn't tell."

That's because his movie choices probably end at the *Die Hard* series. The printer behind me finally stops, and I grab the rest of the notes from the paper tray. "Here you go." I hand them to Detective Lange.

Nolan comes out of my office and gives me an almost imperceptible nod to let me know he was successful with his call.

Detective Lange turns on his heel and starts for the door.

"You're welcome!" I call after him.

Nolan rubs my back. "Sorry about him."

"Stop apologizing for him. What he does or doesn't do is not a reflection on you in any way."

"Thanks, Doc." He kisses my temple.

"So, when's dinner?" I ask.

"Actually, Annabelle suggested we come for Sunday brunch instead. And I made sure to tell her I'd like to make this a surprise. Like you said, she was happy that I wanted to improve my relationship with Drew."

"Perfect."

"Yeah, except Annabelle was so excited I felt awful for lying to her."

"*Did* you lie?" I ask. I can tell Nolan does wish he had a better relationship with his brother. Drew is the one who caused this feud. All because he resented the fact that his parents had a second child. And the ten-year age gap didn't help bring them together at all.

He bobs one shoulder. "Is it weird that I'm kind of looking forward to brunch tomorrow?"

"Not at all." I'm sure I'm part of the reason that Drew is so awful to Nolan these days. I didn't exactly help the situation any.

"Do you want to call it a day on this investigation?"

I want to pour over my notes more so I'm prepared for tomorrow. "Do you mind if I go home and read through my notes some more? I really want to be able to talk things through with Drew at brunch."

"Are you ditching me?" he asks, pressing a hand to his chest in mock hurt.

"Is that awful?"

He places his hands on my waist. "No. I have an article to work on anyway. I'll drive you home."

"Thank you."

Once I'm home and settled in for the rest of the evening, I heat up some leftover soup in my refrigerator and sit down at the kitchen table with my notebook. The notes I gave Detective Lange are more in-depth because they include my interpretation of things Donna told me. The notebook in front of me contains Donna's raw emotions and things she said. That's what I'd rather focus on in case I read anything differently into our conversations now that she's dead. There's a good chance my perception of things has changed.

Donna spent most of her time focused on her fears. Sometimes, she talked about them as if she wanted to get over them but didn't know how. Other times, she used those fears as a crutch. She liked to complain about other people and how they'd wronged her. In a way, I think it made her feel stronger knowing she was dealing with so much and still pushing through. Of course, there's also the possibility that Donna found fault in everyone around her as a way to make herself feel better about her own flaws.

I'm getting nowhere fast. If my notes were a fiction novel, I'd say I had an unreliable narrator on my hands. I can't believe anything Donna told me. And even though I wrote these notes myself, they still seem like nothing but lies.

But the thing about lies is that they're usually rooted in truth. I just have to figure out how to uncover it.

Chapter Six

Nolan and I ring the doorbell of Drew and Annabelle Lange's house at exactly ten o'clock on Sunday morning. I could barely sleep last night between pouring over my notes and anticipating Drew's reaction to Nolan and me coming to brunch this morning.

The front door opens, and Drew's face is the picture of shock. "No." He starts to close the door, but Annabelle appears behind him.

"Sweetheart, let them in. It's cold outside."

Drew grimaces as he opens the door again.

"Thank you," I say, plastering a smile on my face. "I brought some scones. I hope that's okay." I hold up the covered dish in my hands.

"Oh, how lovely. Thank you." Annabelle takes the dish from me. "Drew, say hello to your brother," she calls over her shoulder as she leads me to the kitchen.

Drew doesn't say a word as he closes the front door.

"It smells great in here," Nolan tells Annabelle.

"We've been cooking all morning," she says.

"Yes, I thought we were having friends over," Drew says, finally speaking.

"Better than that," Annabelle says, placing my dish on the counter and turning to Drew. "Surprise!" She smiles widely. "Isn't this great? Nolan wants to spend time with you."

Drew glares at Nolan. "Great," he forces out between clenched teeth.

"With both our jobs, we haven't had time to reconnect," Nolan says, and my heart breaks a little because I can tell how much Nolan would like to change things between them.

"Sit, sit," Annabelle says.

"Let me help you with the food," I say, moving toward the counter.

Annabelle and I place all the serving dishes on the table and sit down. She already has the coffee and orange juice poured. She really went all out with pancakes, waffles, eggs, bacon, sausage, and home fries. I didn't need to bring blueberry scones, but I didn't want to come emptyhanded.

"Dig in," she says, reaching for the dish of bacon and handing it to Drew.

We each fill our plates.

"So, Drew," I say, knowing it's going to annoy him that I'm not calling him Detective, but then again, he refuses to call me Doctor. "Did you have a chance to read through my notes from my sessions with Donna?"

"He was reading them all evening." Annabelle turns to him. "What time were you up until? One? Two?"

"I don't know. It was late." Drew shoves a piece of bacon into his mouth and avoids looking at anyone.

"I'm sure you noticed that Donna didn't like to mention anyone in her life by name," I say.

Drew simply nods.

"I'm tossing around the theory that she was testing me to see if I was trustworthy."

Still nothing from Drew.

"She was definitely holding back in our sessions. What do you make of that?" I ask so he can't continue to ignore me.

"You're the psychologist. You tell me," he says.

"She just did," Annabelle says. "She thinks the woman was testing her. I think Sydney is asking for your opinion about that." She sips her orange juice, and I smile at her.

"That's exactly what I'm asking," I say.

"I think our opinions don't matter. We're searching for a killer."

This isn't working. I need to try a new tactic. "She complained about a lot of people in her life. I'm questioning if the problem was really with everyone else or if Donna liked to stir up trouble." I pause and stare at Drew, who sips his coffee as if I'm not even talking.

"According to Donna's ex-boyfriend, she didn't get along with her neighbor."

Silence.

"Drew, Sydney is speaking to you. You're being rude," Annabelle says.

Nolan tosses his napkin onto the table. "It's okay, Annabelle. This is just my brother. He's never going to change."

Drew puts down his mug and looks at Nolan. "You think I don't know what you're trying to pull here?"

"What are you talking about?" Annabelle asks.

"This." Drew pounds his fist on the table. "Nolan doesn't care about getting to know me better. All he cares about is solving this case and making me look bad."

Annabelle shakes her head.

"This was my idea, not Nolan's," I say. "You want the truth, Drew?"

He won't even look at me.

"I need your help. There. Are you happy now? I admitted I can't solve this case on my own."

"Why would you solve the case?" Annabelle asks. "You're not a detective."

"No. She's a nosey woman who thinks she can do my job better than I can because she got lucky figuring out a couple cases."

"If you remember, I only got involved in that first case because you accused me of a murder I didn't commit."

"Okay, I think everyone should take a few deep breaths," Annabelle says.

"No, let's get this all out in the open." Drew points a finger in Nolan's face. "You blame me for being such an awful brother, but you have no idea how much I lost the day you were born."

"Drew!" Annabelle shrieks.

"It's okay," Nolan says. "Let him talk. I want to hear this." He faces Drew. "What did you lose?"

"My parents. They'd tried to have another baby for years but couldn't. Do you have any idea how that made me feel?"

"Like you weren't good enough," I say, picking up on it immediately.

Drew's gaze flicks to me, but he doesn't confirm anything.

"Ten years. Ten years of watching Mom cry over how she'd never have another child. And then they found out she was pregnant. The doctors said the pregnancy was high risk because of Mom's age, so she spent the entire nine months in bed. I had no mother during that time, and Dad was working around the clock trying to make extra money for the new baby. I had no one. I had to make my own meals, struggle through homework on my own…" He can't get the rest of his sentence out.

"That must have been awful," I say.

"Don't," he chokes out. "I don't want your pity."

"I'm not pitying you. I still think you're wrong."

He opens his mouth to lash out at me, but I don't give him the chance.

"What happened to you is undeniably awful, but it's not Nolan's fault."

"After he was born, it got worse," Drew says. "He was the miracle baby." He practically spits the words. "They fawned over him. Gave him everything I never had."

"Drew, I didn't know," Nolan says.

Of course, Nolan wouldn't know that. He was too young to remember.

"You moved out at eighteen. I was eight years old. All I remember is that you hated me."

Annabelle wipes a tear that escapes her eye. "I'm so sorry for you both." She places her hand on top of Drew's and squeezes it. To my surprise, he doesn't pull away. He really loves her, and she's probably the only person in the world he trusts.

"It doesn't matter now." Drew drinks his orange juice.

He would really benefit from a few sessions in my office, but I don't dare suggest it since I'm high up on his list of people he doesn't like. "I have an idea."

Nolan must be afraid I'm going to suggest therapy because his face goes completely pale.

"I think we can all solve this case together. Why don't we pool our resources and figure out who killed Donna Barrett?" I say, hoping to put everyone at ease.

"That's a great idea," Annabelle says. I can tell she's hoping this will get the two brothers to work together and get along. I'm not as optimistic this will fix everything, but I do think it will help break the ice.

Drew is quiet, so I can't tell how he feels about the idea. Nolan looks at him, and it breaks my heart to see how much he wants his older brother to accept him.

"I'm curious if there are records at the SCPD of Donna calling to complain about her neighbor," I say, trying to get the ball rolling.

Annabelle holds her coffee mug in both hands and looks at Drew. "Drew? You can easily find that out, right?"

He clears his throat. "I can." He raises his gaze to me. "What else do you have?"

"Donna had a friend named Cara. According to Donna's ex-boyfriend, Pierce, Cara tried to push Donna to get over some of her fears."

"You think that's who convinced her to go to the haunted house," Drew says, and it's not a question.

I nod. "I don't know her last name. I haven't had a chance to look into her too much."

Drew bobs his head.

"Sweetie, tell Sydney and Nolan what you found out," Annabelle says.

Nolan and I look at Drew. He doesn't appear eager to share, but now that Annabelle has seen us give Drew information, she's not going to let him get away with withholding information from us. My plan for this meal together is working out exactly as I'd hoped.

"One of the kids at the youth center also works at the food store. Shop Smart. Apparently, Donna thought he was stalking her while she shopped."

Oh boy. This is not going to go over well with Autumn and Aaron. I thought Drew only asked for the list of kids at the youth center to throw Nolan and me off the real trail he was pursuing, but if he does suspect one of them, this could get bad, and quickly.

"Who is it?" I ask. "I know most of the kids there."

"Neil Thatcher," Drew says, and I can tell he's studying me for a reaction to the name.

"He's not a legal adult yet," I say.

"I know. I have to bring him in to the station and have his parents present when I question him."

I want to be there, but I know Drew won't react well to me asking. However, now is the time to ask. Hopefully, Annabelle will back me up. "I think it might help if you have me there during the questioning. It might make Neil's parents feel more comfortable."

"That's not a bad idea," Annabelle says.

"I can't see the chief going along with that," Drew says.

"Then don't question Neil at the station."

Nolan nods to back me up. "Syd is right. If we go to Neil's house, he'll be on his own turf. It will be less intimidating for him."

"Sometimes being intimidating is a good thing," Drew says. "If this kid killed Donna Barrett, I want him to know I'm going to catch him."

Annabelle places one hand on Drew's forearm. "He's just a kid."

"He's sixteen. He's plenty capable of murder."

He doesn't know Neil. I can't say I know him very well either. He's quiet and pretty well built. I'd guess he lifts weights or something along those lines. Of course, Neil's physique could be what's leading Drew to believing the kid could have killed Donna. However, she was surprised in the dark. I don't think it would have taken all that much strength to kill her. Anyone could have done it.

"I have some patients who are underage. The key is to make sure their parents feel comfortable with you. If you don't, they're going to lawyer up," I say.

Drew seems to give that some thought. "I suppose questioning him at his house is a good idea. It will let me get a better feel for the type of person Neil is as well."

If I could see Neil's room, that would probably help. I'm not sure he or his parents would invite me to look around, though. "We'd really like to help you."

Annabelle squeezes Drew's arm. "Sweetie, can I talk to you in the other room for a moment?"

Drew puts his fork down on his plate and stands up.

"Excuse us," Annabelle says with a smile.

Once they're out of the kitchen, I take Nolan's hand in mine. "How are you holding up?" It's tough to be the caring girlfriend without coming across as a psychologist who is reading into his every move.

"I'm not expecting miracles, Syd. Drew is Drew. He's not going to change overnight, if ever. I have to accept that."

"No, you don't. You can keep trying. Make him see that he's missing out on having a great brother in his life. I don't think it's too late for you two to patch things up. It's going to take time and a lot of hard work, though."

"I'm not sure he wants me in his life. I never knew my parents did that to him. I feel terrible. And even though I know it's not my fault, I don't see how being around me can be easy for him."

Out of the corner of my eye, I see Drew and Annabelle walking back into the kitchen, but I purposely pretend to be so caught up talking to Nolan that I don't notice. "The reality of the situation is that you're both victims here. Your parents created a divide between you two, but you can repair it. Don't let them win by not getting to know your brother."

Annabelle loops her arm through Drew's. "Did you hear what Sydney said? She's right, Drew. Your parents created this problem, and by not fixing it, you and Nolan are letting them get away with it."

"I'm sorry. I didn't realize you were back," I say, tucking a strand of hair behind my ear and feigning innocence.

"No, it's good we heard you," Annabelle says. "This needs to end."

Nolan stands up. "Look, Drew, I understand how you feel, and I know we're not going to fix this in a day, but I'd really like to help you with this case. Who knows? Maybe we'll find out we can get along and make a good team."

"What do you say, sweetie?" Annabelle asks him.

Drew takes a deep breath. "I'll call the Thatchers and set up a meeting with them tomorrow. I'll be in touch with the details. You can meet me there."

Annabelle clasps her hands together and smiles, a tear trailing down her cheek. Drew's gesture isn't a brotherly hug or anything like that, but I think it's the best we can ask from him right now.

"Thank you," Nolan says. "And Annabelle, thank you for this delicious brunch."

"I'll help you clean up," I say.

"I'll help her clean up. You two are free to go." Drew is dismissing us. It's clear we've pushed him to his limit this morning, and he needs time to process.

"Of course," I say, standing up and taking Nolan's hand. "Annabelle, thank you for everything."

She looks like she wants to hug me and Nolan, but she wraps her arms around Drew instead. The tension in his body eases at her touch. He's fortunate he found someone who can see past his rough exterior. There's definitely something special about Annabelle.

"I'll walk you to the door," she says, and Drew immediately begins clearing the table.

"Goodbye, Drew," Nolan says.

"Detective," I say with a nod to him.

His only reply is a curt nod as he carries a stack of dishes to the sink.

Nolan and I put on our coats at the front door.

"He'll come around," Annabelle tells us in a whisper. "I really think this is going to be good for him."

I loop my arm through Nolan's. "For both of them," I say.

"Take care," Annabelle says as we walk outside.

"I like her," Nolan says.

"I do, too."

Once we're on the way to my house, my phone rings. "It's Autumn," I tell Nolan before answering. "Hey, Autumn. I was going to call you."

"Syd, it's Kevin."

"What about Kevin?"

"He's missing."

Chapter Seven

"Missing? How do you know?"

"I called him this morning to make sure he was okay after Detective Lange questioned him yesterday. He didn't answer, so I went to his apartment. His landlord said he heard a noise in the middle of the night. He said it sounded like someone running down the hallway and down the stairs. He went to find out what was going on, but he didn't see anything."

"You think Kevin ran away?" I ask.

Nolan eyes me for a moment before focusing on the road again.

"His apartment door was unlocked. I tried it on instinct. Kevin isn't the type of person to leave his door unlocked. He's an eighteen-year-old kid living on his own."

"Do you think he was kidnapped?" I ask.

"I don't know what to think."

"Where are you now?"

"At the laundromat under his apartment. I'm asking around to see if anyone saw him."

"Laundromat," I tell Nolan. "Autumn, we're on our way."

"Good because Aaron is at that youth center. He's checking in with the other kids to see if anyone knows where Kevin might be."

Smart. If Kevin did take off, there's a chance he told one of his friends there. Of course, there's also a good chance that friend would cover for him. "Do you want us to call Detective Lange?"

"We don't know if this is a missing persons situation. I don't think the police will do anything about it yet. We don't even know how long he's been gone."

She's right. They'd probably give us a line about how Kevin went out to run errands or something. We have no way of knowing when he really disappeared or if he went on his own accord. Until we know something, we can't involve the police.

"We'll be there soon," I tell her before ending the call.

"Should I call Drew?" Nolan asks me.

"I think Drew needs some space right now. Let's see what we can figure out first. We can always call him after we check out Kevin's place."

Nolan turns down Main Street, heading for the laundromat. Since it's a weekend, the place is pretty packed. I spot Autumn's car and point it out to Nolan. He parks as close to it as possible given the number of cars in the lot. We go inside, and I find Autumn at the counter. Knowing her, she wanted to stay close to someone who works here so she can question them and everyone who comes in to drop off or pick up their clothing.

"Hey." I give her a hug. "You okay?"

"No one's seen him."

"All right. Let's go up to his apartment," I say. If the door is open, and the landlord isn't watching, we can go inside and look for any signs that Kevin didn't leave on his own.

Autumn points to the stairs. "Over there."

We walk up to the second floor. It looks like there are six apartments.

"The one on the end here is the landlord's."

Right by the stairs, which is why he heard the commotion last night. I press a finger to my lips in case the landlord is home. I don't want him coming out here and stopping us from going inside Kevin's apartment. I mouth, "Which one is Kevin's?" to Autumn.

She walks to the door, takes a deep breath, and opens it.

The apartment is a studio. There's a murphy bed, which is currently open. The sheets look slept in, but Kevin is an eighteen-year-old boy living on his own, so it's entirely possible that he never makes his bed.

Since the apartment is so small, it won't take us long to check out the entire space. Nolan closes the door behind us so no one knows we're here without permission.

There's a four-drawer dresser in the wall by the bed. I walk over to it and open the top drawer. Most of the contents of the drawer are missing. That or Kevin barely had any belongings to his name.

"I've never actually been inside the apartment like this before," Autumn says. "I mean I've dropped him off, and I opened the door earlier when I discovered Kevin was missing, but now that I'm fully taking it in and seeing how he lives…" Her words are cut off by sobs. "The poor kid. First his parents are killed, and then he's forced to live in this tiny hole in the wall. He deserves so much better."

Nolan nods to me, and I go to console Autumn while he searches the apartment.

"We're going to find him. After that we'll see what we can do about getting him a better place to live."

"He needs a better job. He works at the laundromat downstairs. They can't be paying him enough to clean the place if this is all he owns. He doesn't even have a TV or anything."

"I promise we'll look in to all of that once we find him, but his safety has to be top priority right now."

She gives me a hug. "I'm trying to figure out where he'd go, but I can't think of anyone he has other than those of us at the youth center."

"Who is he closest to there?" I ask. "Maybe we should go talk to them."

"Probably Mario. He's the oldest after Kevin. They get along well."

"Why don't you call Mario?" I say. "See if he'll either come meet us or if we can go to his house."

She pulls her phone from her back pocket to make the call. I squeeze her arm before going over to Nolan, who is in the bathroom now. I have to stand in the doorway because the space isn't large enough for two people. There's a very small shower stall, a tiny sink, and a toilet. There's standing room for one person in the center of the room.

"Find anything?" I ask.

"Not really. There's nowhere to put anything, so I can't tell if he packed up his things or never had any to begin with."

"Autumn is calling a friend of Kevin's."

"Good. Hopefully, he told someone he was going somewhere."

I can't think of who would want to kidnap a person who has no family or belongings. It couldn't be for a ransom because there's no one to pay it. And I highly doubt this place was robbed before Kevin disappeared. Kevin clearly had nothing, and who would even think to rob a studio apartment above a laundromat? It doesn't add up.

I go to the kitchen and open the refrigerator, which looks to be at least twenty years old. The light bulb inside is out, but the only food—a carton of milk and a half-eaten loaf of bread—are still visible in the dark. I quickly close the door before Autumn can get upset by this, too.

I turn to Nolan and shake my head. This hasn't been helpful in the least.

Autumn ends her call and walks over to us in the kitchen. "Mario said he'd meet us at the youth center."

Detective Lange won't like that, but I can see why Mario feels comfortable meeting us there.

"You drive with Autumn," Nolan says. "I'll meet you two there."

He's so sweet for realizing Autumn needs me right now.

I mouth, "Thank you."

He gives me a quick kiss before we walk out of the apartment.

I hold out my hand to Autumn. "Keys. I'll drive."

She hands over her car keys without protest. Autumn isn't big on driving to begin with. She actually hates it.

As I drive us to the youth center, I get an idea. "Hey, Kevin is an adult now, and he knows the youth center really well. Is it in your budget to hire him?"

She grabs my arms so quickly and tightly I jump. "Syd, that is the best idea ever. I could totally hire him. And we even have a small apartment space in the back. It's barely bigger than where he's living now, but it would only be temporary to help him get back on his feet. He could stay there to save money and avoid paying rent for a while. Then he should be able to afford a bigger place after maybe a year or so."

I turn to smile at her. "I think he'll really like that plan."

She looks down at her hands, which are now clenched in her lap. "Great. Now we just have to find him and hope he's okay."

"I'm sure he is." I'm lying. I have no idea what happened to Kevin, but for Autumn's sake, I have to believe he got scared and ran.

I park in Autumn's spot at the youth center. Nolan beat us there, and he's waiting outside his car. He walks over to us, wrapping one arm around my waist. Autumn heads inside first, with us right behind her.

"She looks better."

"We came up with a plan to have Kevin live and work at the youth center for a while so he can save up some money."

"That's a great idea. And if he needs extra work, I can see if there's anything at the paper for him to do. He used to clean the laundromat, right?"

I nod. "Okay, I'll talk to Mr. Burke and see if there's anything Kevin can do."

"Thank you."

Aaron comes out of the office when he hears us. "Hey." He hugs Autumn. "Mario is in the game room waiting for you. He got here a few minutes ago."

"Did he say anything to you?" Autumn asks as we walk toward the game room.

"No, and I didn't want to push him. He seems scared."

Autumn opens the door, and Mario jumps at the creaking sound it makes. "It's only us," she reassures him.

We need him to calm down, so I point to the pool stick he's holding in his hands. "Want to play a game while we talk?"

"You play?" he asks me.

"Why do you sound like you're having a hard time believing that?"

He shrugs. "You're a doctor."

"Ouch. I'm not sure how to take that. You make it sound like such a bad thing."

"Nah. You're cool."

"Thanks. So what do you say? Play me? We can make it interesting. If you win, I'll have your favorite meal delivered to you."

"And if you win?" he asks. "I don't have much money."

"Oh, now you think I might actually be able to play?"

He looks down at the table and bobs one shoulder. "I can't afford to take the chance if money is on the line."

"Okay, how about this? If I win, you have to help Autumn and Aaron out around here for a day after the place can reopen."

He cocks his head. "How come you don't get anything in this deal?"

"I do. Autumn is my best friend. I'm happy when she's happy." He bobs his head.

"Is that how it is with you and Kevin?" I grab a pool stick and chalk the tip, hoping he doesn't realize I'm trying to form a common ground for us so he'll open up to me.

"What do you mean?" He starts racking the balls.

"You two help each other out, right?"

"Are you asking if I helped him disappear?"

"Did you?" I wait for him to finish racking the balls and gesture for me to break. I line-up my shot. It's not the best break in the world, but I get two striped balls in the corner pockets. "I'm stripes."

"Kevin called me last night. He was freaked out after that cop questioned him."

"I tried to help him out during that," I say.

"I know. He told me."

"The police don't think Kevin killed that woman." I want to make sure Mario knows that so he can relay the message to Kevin. Maybe that will make Kevin feel safe enough to come home.

"They don't?"

I take my next shot, but I miss. "Your turn."

He leans down to line up his shot, aiming for the two ball. "Kevin said it looked bad that he was in the asylum room right before the body was found and that the woman was stabbed. He was the only one working the haunted house who had a knife."

"A fake knife," I say. "Hardly the murder weapon."

He makes his shot and lines up another. "Yeah, but he figures the cops think he swapped out the fake knife for a real one without anyone knowing." He makes the second shot, too.

"I feel like I'm being hustled here," I say, examining the balls on the table.

Mario shakes his head. "We're tied right now."

"Why would anyone think Kevin had a reason to kill Donna Barrett? They didn't even know each other, did they?"

Mario misses his next shot, and I suspect it's because my question distracted him. He knows something. Something that might make Kevin look suspicious.

"Mario, is there a reason why someone might think Kevin would harm Donna Barrett?"

"It's your shot," he says, ignoring my question.

I check out what shots I have lined up. I sink two balls in a row and miss the third on purpose. "You're up," I say, hoping he realizes I mean it's time for him to answer my question.

He narrows his eyes at me. "Did you miss your shot on purpose?"

"Are you avoiding my question on purpose?"

He makes three shots in a row before standing up to face me again. "If I tell you this, and you go to the police, they're going to search for him."

How bad can this be? "Mario, I don't think Kevin harmed Donna in any way."

"Yeah, but that detective guy is his brother." He points his pool stick at Nolan.

Nolan holds up both hands. "I'm not going to report back to my brother. We don't exactly have that kind of relationship." As much as Nolan is trying to help, his tone makes it clear he wishes he did have that relationship with Drew.

And it's not like I can ask Nolan to leave the room. Mario knows we're a couple, so he'd assume I'd fill Nolan in as soon as I was able to. "Mario, do you believe Kevin is innocent?" I ask.

"Of course. He's no killer."

I gesture to Autumn, Aaron, and Nolan. "Well, we all believe the same thing, and we're trying to prove it, but if we don't know everything, the police might blindside us with something. We need all the information if we're going to protect Kevin. There can't be any surprises. Do you understand what I'm saying?"

He looks at Nolan. "You swear you're not going to run to your brother or write about this for the paper?"

"You have my word."

Mario is quiet while he finishes cleaning up all the solids on the table. He puts his pool stick back on the rack on the wall. "I want fried shrimp and strip steak from Red Lobster."

"Done," I say. "A deal's a deal."

"Really? I thought you'd shoot that down. I had a backup order ready and everything." He's probably thinking I'd assume he'd choose fast food, being that he's a teenager.

"I keep my word, Mario. We all do. That's who we are. I mean think about it. Would Autumn and Aaron run this place if they didn't want to help people? Would I be a therapist? Would Nolan dedicate his life to keeping the public informed of the truth?"

"In other words, I should trust you guys," he says.

"We're really trying to help Kevin, but we need you in order to do that."

He lets out a deep breath, and his shoulders sag. "Donna Barrett complained about Kevin to his boss at the laundromat. I guess he washed the floor and didn't put up the caution sign fast enough for her. She was dropping off some dry cleaning, and she slipped. She wasn't hurt, but she demanded he be fired. He lost his job early last week because of her."

My heart nearly sinks to my stomach. That job was Kevin's only source of income. Without it, he'd lose the little he had. The police are definitely going to see this as motive for revenge.

Chapter Eight

Now I see why Mario was hesitant to talk in front of Nolan. Detective Drew Lange would definitely put out a BOLO on Kevin. He would want to find him and bring him back in for questioning.

I meet Nolan's gaze, and he shakes his head.

"This is what we're going to do," Nolan says. "No one acknowledges this conversation ever happened. We need to find Kevin and bring him home so we can make sure he's safe. There's a chance the police will find out Donna got Kevin fired from the laundromat, so we need to get him a new job immediately so he doesn't look suspicious."

"Done," Autumn says. "We'll hire him here. We can say he was already working for us by Friday night."

Aaron nods. "That's one problem solved. If Kevin had already recovered from losing that job, he'd have no reason to harm Donna Barrett."

"And he needs to move in here as soon as we find him," Autumn says. "That way it won't look suspicious that he packed up his apartment above the laundromat."

Except Autumn is the one who questioned the landlord about Kevin's whereabouts. If Detective Lange finds that out, we're back at square one. He'll never believe Autumn forgot she let Kevin move into the youth center. "There's still the problem that we went looking for Kevin," I say.

"She's right." Nolan leans on the pool table.

"I can say he crashed with me for the night before coming here," Mario says.

I don't like that. I don't want Mario lying to the police. "No. I don't want you getting involved," I tell Mario. Kevin doesn't have any family, so we can't claim he went to visit a relative. And he doesn't have a car, so we can't say he slept there either.

"I could say I forgot to tell Autumn I gave Kevin the room here," Aaron says. "We have a lot going on. The police might believe it slipped my mind, and Autumn didn't know about it."

"Maybe, but we'd need to find Kevin fast and get him into the apartment here if we're going to pull this off." I look to Mario. "Do you have any idea where he might go?"

"He wouldn't get far on foot."

"He could have taken the trolley or the bus," Nolan says.

"But to where?" I ask.

"He loves the beach," Mario says.

"Which one?" I ask.

"Lewes. He thinks Rehoboth is too crowded."

Would he sleep on the beach? I'd think the police would pick him up for that. "Mario, can you call him?"

"I've already tried. He isn't answering."

"Try texting him to tell him that we're going to help him, but we need to bring him back in order to do it."

"I can pick him up wherever he is," Aaron says. "Since he's an employee now, no one would think anything of me driving him here."

I bob my head. "Can you do that, Mario?"

He takes his phone from his back pocket, and his thumbs fly across the screen. "Done. There's no saying if he'll reply, though." His phone dings the second he gets the words out. "Wait. He says he wants to talk to Aaron."

"Tell him to call your phone. Let him know you're with me," Aaron says.

Mario sends the text, and about thirty seconds later, his phone rings. "Man, you had us all worried. We figured it out, though. We're going to get you out of this mess. Hold on. Aaron's right here." He hands the phone to Aaron, who puts the call on speaker so we all can hear.

"Kevin, it's Aaron. Long story short, Autumn and I hired you right after you lost your job at the laundromat. You've been working for us all week. And we're going to let you stay in the apartment in the youth center."

"Rent free," Autumn adds. "We know you're innocent, Kevin. Please just let us bring you back. Nothing is going to happen to you. I promise."

"That detective doesn't like me. He's going to bring me to the station when he finds out she got me fired."

"No, he won't," Nolan says. "Kevin, this is Nolan Lange. I will make sure my brother steers clear of you in this investigation."

"How? You two don't even like each other."

"We've sort of made a truce. Besides, he has another suspect he's looking into."

"Who?" Kevin asks.

"I can't tell you that, and I think it's best if you stay as far away from the investigation as possible."

I move toward the phone. "Kevin, it's Sydney. Let Aaron come get you. You have friends here. We're going to protect you."

"We're your family, Kevin," Autumn says. "Please let us bring you home."

There's silence for about fifteen seconds. "Okay. I'm at the park in Lewes."

He must have taken the trolley there. It's smart. There are bathrooms and plenty of places to seek shelter.

"I'm leaving now. Meet me by the restrooms," Aaron says. He hands the phone back to Mario.

"Be safe, man," Mario says before ending the call.

Aaron and Autumn say goodbye and hurry out of the youth center. I don't have the heart to tell them another one of their kids is going to be questioned by Detective Lange tomorrow. They have enough to deal with right now, and Nolan and I will be present when Drew talks to Neil Thatcher.

I call in Mario's dinner order before we leave the youth center and have it delivered to him at his house.

"You didn't have to buy me dinner," he says as we walk out of the youth center. "I appreciate that you're helping Kevin. That's more than enough."

"You won, and like I said, I'm true to my word."

"I believe you. Thanks." He gives us a brief nod before walking toward the bus stop.

"Hey, do you want a ride?" Nolan calls after him.

Mario shakes his head. "Nah. I'm good."

I get the feeling he doesn't want us to see where he lives. He seems ashamed of where he comes from and how little he has. His phone is probably his only possession of value. I really have to hand it to Autumn and Aaron. They're doing so much for these kids.

Nolan drives me back to my place, and we have a nice home-cooked meal. He grills steak and vegetable kabobs on the back patio while I make German potato salad. We sit down at the table and dig in, both of us starving. Autumn texts us once Kevin is back at the youth center and settled into his room. She said he was really scared and still is, but he trusts them.

Now as long as Nolan and I can keep Drew off Kevin's trail, things should work out fine from here. Speaking of Drew, he texts Nolan around eight o'clock when we're sitting in the living room enjoying some wine after a long day.

"Drew texted me." Nolan stares at the message.

"Is everything okay?" I ask, not wanting to read over his shoulder.

"Yeah, it's just that he's never texted me before. Ever."

I place my hand on his leg and gently squeeze. "What does it say?"

Nolan clears his throat, and I suspect it's to remove the lump that's formed there. "He says we're going to meet at Neil's house at nine o'clock tomorrow morning."

"I guess his parents are going into work late so they can be present."

"Seems that way, but Nolan didn't actually say."

Baby steps. I wonder how long it took Annabelle to convince Drew to text Nolan. I don't think patching up thirty-one years of a bad relationship will be easy.

Nolan picks me up at a quarter to nine so we can drive to Neil Thatcher's house. After Nolan left last night, I did some digging online and found out Neil lives with foster parents. He was given up for adoption at birth. He got tossed around from home to home for years, and now he's with a foster family. It's awful what some kids have to endure in life. What ever happened to having a childhood?

Neil's foster house is in a big development where the houses are packed together so tightly no one has an actual yard. His house is centrally located with other houses on all sides. I'm not sure who came up with this design, but I'm pretty sure their only concern was cramming in as many houses as they possibly could. Aesthetics had nothing to do with it.

We park in front of the white house and walk up to the door. Detective Lange's patrol car is here, so he must be inside already. Nolan rings the bell. A woman with graying hair pulled up into a messy bun answers the door.

"Hi, we're—"

She waves us inside. "I know who you are. The reporter and the shrink. Come on in. It's cold out there."

We step inside, and she immediately closes the door behind us. Then she pulls her long cardigan tightly around her body. "In the kitchen," she says, pointing us in the direction.

As soon as we enter the room, Drew raises his gaze to us from his seat at the kitchen table. Neil is seated across from him.

"Tea?" the woman asks us. I'm assuming she's the foster mother, Camille Jeffrey.

"No, thank you," Nolan says, and I shake my head.

"I was just getting started," Detective Lange says. "Neil was telling me why Donna Barrett took out a restraining order against him."

Nolan and I sit down at the table. Camilla stands at the sink with her mug of tea in her hands.

"I never followed her around. I don't know why she thought I did. I was doing my job. I stock the shelves. You can ask my boss. I go where I'm told to go. They give me boxes of things to shelve. I have no control over it or over who happens to be shopping in the aisle at the time." Neil blurts it all out in one breath.

"Relax, Neil. It's okay," I say.

"The one time, I asked my supervisor if I could work in a different aisle because I saw Ms. Barrett in the laundry detergent aisle and I didn't want to be near her. He told me to do my job and stop complaining. I didn't want to get fired, so I went back to the aisle and worked without looking at her."

"What did she do?" I ask.

"She marched over to me and said I came back into the aisle because she was there. I told her I only came back because I was told to."

"How did she react to that?" Detective Lange asks, jotting this all into his notepad.

"She got mad. She said I was lying. Said I was always looking at her inappropriately." Neil meets my gaze. "No offense or anything, but she was more than twice my age. I wasn't looking at her inappropriately at all."

"What happened after that?" Detective Lange presses.

"She started yelling, made a big scene. I kept working. I didn't know what else to do. But then my boss came by, and Ms. Barrett said she wanted me fired."

"Did your boss fire you?" I ask.

He nods. "I think he thought it was the only way to get her to stop screaming. But afterward, he told me I could keep my job as long as I stayed in the back room when she was inside the store."

"Was anyone else in the aisle at the time?" Detective Lange asks.

"Yeah, there was this other lady. She stuck up for me. Told my boss I was minding my own business, doing my job, and Ms. Barrett started going off on me for no reason." He leans back in his chair. "Then they started yelling at each other."

"Do you know who the woman was?" I ask.

He shakes his head. "I didn't have time to ask either or to thank her. My boss told me to get my things and leave. I don't know what happened after that."

"I read the police report," Detective Lange says. "Donna Barrett took out a restraining order against you."

"Yeah, she did."

"But you can't think of any reason why she'd do that? Did something happen prior to that day that would have caused her to believe you were dangerous to her in some way?"

Neil shakes his head. "I'm a good worker. I swear I was just doing my job."

Detective Lange bobs his head. "Did you ever see Ms. Barrett after that?"

Neil's chest rises but doesn't fall. He's holding his breath. "At the haunted house. I was working it with the others from the youth center. I wasn't in the asylum room, though. I was stationed at the exit. I was wearing a big hairy gorilla suit."

If he was dressed as a gorilla, I doubt he'd be able to slink around undetected even in the dark.

"Okay, I'll follow up to check that someone can verify your location at the time of the murder."

"Were you with anyone?" I ask.

"Mario."

"I know him," I say. "I can talk to him to verify your alibi for you."

Neil nods. "Look, I don't know why that lady hated me, but I'd never kill anyone." His gaze flits to Camille, who is on her phone now. Neil leans forward and lowers his voice. "Being in foster care is bad enough. I definitely don't want to go to jail."

I give Detective Lange a discreet nod to let him know I believe Neil is telling us the truth.

Detective Lange pulls a card from his inside jacket pocket. "If you think of anything else, give me a call."

Neil picks up the card. "Yeah, okay."

The three of us stand up, leaving Neil at the table alone.

"Hey," he calls after us. "Do you guys have any idea who killed her?"

"Thank you for your time," Detective Lange says, dismissing the question as he heads for the door.

I meet Neil's gaze and shake my head before following the brothers out of the house. Camille doesn't even acknowledge us.

"What do you think?" Nolan asks Drew as we approach our cars.

"I think he's not telling us something. There has to be a reason Donna Barrett thought Neil was a threat to her."

"Do you think Neil was lying?" I ask. "Because I didn't pick up on any cues that usually point to someone being dishonest or even withholding information."

"Honestly, I'm not sure. All I know is something set her off."

"What's your next step then?" Nolan asks.

"I'm going to talk to Cara Romney. That's the friend Donna went to the haunted house with."

Oh, good. He managed to find her. "Do you mind if we tag along?" I ask. "I actually have quite a bit I'd like to ask Cara."

Detective Lange crosses his arms. "I let you come with me on this one, but you're not detectives. I can't bring you to interrogate every suspect I have."

"Why not?" I ask. "I'm sure Annabelle would agree it's a good idea."

"Annabelle isn't here," he says lowering his arms and glaring at me.

"No problem." I remove my phone from my back pocket. "I'll give her a quick call."

"Syd, I don't think that's helping," Nolan says, placing his hand on top of my phone.

In reality, I couldn't call her anyway. I don't have her number. Nolan does. But Detective Lange doesn't know that.

"Drew, we're offering you free help. Why wouldn't you take it?" Nolan asks him.

"Because I don't need help. I don't need anything from you." He turns on his heel and gets into his patrol car.

Nolan's head falls. I feel bad for him, but we also don't have time to waste.

I nudge his arm with my elbow. "Come on. We have a police detective to tail."

Chapter Nine

To his credit, Nolan recovers quickly from his brother dismissing any relationship they might have. He gets his keys and goes into action. We keep a distance between Detective Lange's patrol car and ours.

"Have you done this before?" I ask Nolan.

"What? Tail someone?"

"Yeah. You're really good at it."

"I've had to tail people before to corner them for interviews. That's the tough part about my job. Most people don't want to talk to the press."

"I didn't consider that. You're probably avoided almost as much as the police in this type of situation."

"Probably. Though there are the few that hope I'll put them on television. Of course, when they find out I'm not a TV reporter, that hope goes out the window and their willingness to speak goes with it."

"I'm sorry." I rest my hand on his leg.

"All par for the course. I knew what I was signing up for with this job."

Still, it must be difficult to constantly have to deal with people running away from you. I have the opposite effect on people. My clients want to pour out every detail of their lives to me. Except for Donna Barrett. Why was she so different? It's like she didn't want to see a psychologist. Maybe her fears made it so difficult to get close to people so she wanted someone to talk to who wouldn't fight back or criticize her. If only I'd known all of this about her when she was still alive. I might have been able to help her, and maybe the person who killed her would have stopped hating her so much and not planned the murder.

"You okay?" Nolan asks.

"Yeah, it's just I think I was in a similar situation with Donna Barrett. There was so much she wouldn't tell me."

He gives me a quick sideways glance. "You're questioning if you could have helped her if she'd been more forthright with you."

"It's hard not to."

"I get that. I do. But you have to know that her holding back wasn't your fault."

"Unless I somehow did something to make her not trust me with that information."

"From what I've gathered about Donna, she didn't get along with very many people in her life at all. Consider yourself part of her inner circle. That's a tough place to get access to. If anything, I'd say you were one of the few people she trusted."

Me and Cara Romney, who was successful in getting Donna to go to the haunted house. But did she convince her to go so she could kill her? We still don't know what happened to Cara at that haunted house. Why was she separated from Donna? Where was she after Donna's body was discovered? It's like she fled, and that spells guilty to me.

Detective Lange's patrol car pulls into a private community. Nolan slows down, letting him get even more of a lead on us. It won't be difficult to spot a patrol car in someone's driveway, so we're not concerned about losing him at this point.

"He went down that road there," I say, motioning to the road on our left. "Drive past it. We don't want him to see us."

Nolan passes the road and drives around the development a few times. "I wonder how long this will take."

We definitely want Detective Lange to be gone before we talk to Cara Romney. He won't like that we tailed him here or that we're questioning his suspects.

"Why don't you park at that cul de sac there? We'll be able to see Cara's driveway and know when Drew leaves."

Nolan bobs his head and follows my advice. He leaves the engine running so we can swoop in once Drew is gone.

My phone rings, and I pull it from my pocket. Autumn's face fills the screen. "Hey, Autumn," I answer.

"Syd, Aaron is back with Kevin. We're getting him set up in the small apartment here. Is Detective Lange with you?"

"Sort of. It depends on how you define the word 'with.'"

"What are you up to?" she asks.

"Well, we questioned Neil Thatcher together."

"What? You questioned Neil, and you didn't tell me?"

I hold up a hand even though she can't see me. "Calm down. Nolan and I insisted on going so we could protect Neil. I didn't tell you because you were already stressed enough about Kevin. I didn't want to add to that. Everything is fine, though. I don't think Detective Lange believes Neil is guilty of anything. Even the restraining order Donna took out on him seems bogus. Neil was only doing his job. Donna's paranoia just led to her misinterpreting the situation."

"No offense, Syd, because I know the woman was one of your clients, but I really don't like her."

"You're not alone there. Most people in her life didn't like her. She seemed to have a problem with everyone except this one friend, Cara Romney. Do you know her?"

"No. Should I?"

"Well, she was at the haunted house Friday night."

"With Donna?"

"At least when they arrived, but Cara seems to have disappeared. She wasn't there when Donna's body was found."

"Interesting. And she's the one who talked Donna into going in the first place, right?"

"You got it. I can tell we're getting the same impression of Cara."

"Yeah, totally suspicious."

"I want to talk to Kevin later, okay?"

"You don't still suspect him, do you?" she asks.

"No, it's more to make sure he's okay."

"Oh, like a free therapy session."

Actually, I want to put Autumn's mind at ease so she knows he'll be okay after all this, but I'd rather not tell her that, so I go with the excuse she gave me. "Yeah, like that."

"Thanks, Syd. That's really sweet of you. I'm sorry I got upset about the Neil thing. I appreciate you and Nolan looking out for him. Neil's a good kid, and I don't think his foster mother cares about him at all. She seems very uninvolved in his life, like her only responsibility is to make sure he has a roof over his head."

"Good thing he has you and Aaron."

"Keep me posted on this Cara woman, okay? I've got to get back to helping Kevin settle in."

"Will do." I end the call.

"She was upset," Nolan says.

"She's fine now. She understands."

"Good. So what kind of things did Donna have to say about Cara in your sessions?"

"Well, it's tough since she didn't name anyone in her life. I'm beginning to think Cara was her only friend though, so going off of that theory, Cara was very outgoing and tried to make Donna outgoing as well. Donna went along with Cara's ideas and plans. I think Donna wanted to use her relationship with Cara to make it seem like she had a good social life, but I don't think that was the case at all."

"How so?"

"Well, I think Donna would tell me about things Cara did but pass it off as if she'd done it."

"What makes you think that?"

"The way she'd explain things. Or rather *not* explain them. She'd give me vague details, and whenever I pushed for more, she'd make up an excuse. Either she wouldn't want to talk about it or she'd claim she was too drunk to remember much of anything."

"But if she was already lying about the experiences being her own, why not lie about the details, too?"

I shrug. "Maybe she was afraid she'd get mixed up about the details if I referred back to them later on." It's how a lot of people get caught in lies. They can't remember every detail of what they lied about, and someone catches them on an inconsistency.

"You know, I actually wouldn't have been surprised if Donna had made up this Cara person."

He makes a good point. Cara could easily have been a figment of Donna's imagination. But Donna's ex-boyfriend Pierce already confirmed Cara is a real person. He's met her. "If not for Pierce telling us about Cara at that beach party, I'd agree with you."

"There's a really good chance that Cara finally got fed up with Donna."

I nod. "Everyone else in Donna's life did. It would make sense."

"That must be what Drew is thinking, too. I'm pretty sure Cara is his top suspect." Nolan looks through the windshield in the direction of Cara's driveway. "What are the odds Drew walks out of the house with Cara in handcuffs?"

"I'd say not bad at all."

We keep an eye on the driveway. Detective Lange is taking an awfully long time in there. Maybe Cara has a lot to say about Donna. I'm eager to get in there and find out for myself. I tap my foot as I count the seconds.

"Try to relax. I know stakeouts aren't exactly fun or entertaining."

"It could be worse," I say. "At least I'm trapped in the car with you."

He smiles at me. "I'm enjoying the company as well, and I'm looking forward to this case being over so you and I can go on real dates again."

"Real dates? What are those?" I tease.

"I guess we should be thankful it's been months since we've been dragged into a murder investigation."

"Yeah, and I'm not the prime suspect. That's definitely a plus."

He laces his fingers through mine and raises our hands to kiss my fingertips. "See. Things aren't so bad."

I'm about to respond when I see Detective Lange walking to his patrol car. Cara isn't with him in handcuffs, which means he either doesn't think she's guilty or doesn't have enough to arrest her. "He's alone," I say.

"I guess that means we'll get to talk to Cara ourselves."

Detective Lange gets into his car and backs out of the driveway. He pauses a little long for merely changing gears from reverse to drive. And when he starts driving away, I can make out the outline of his arm raised as if he's holding his phone to his ear. *Tsk, tsk, Detective. That's what Bluetooth is for.*

Once Detective Lange turns off the road, Nolan drives up to Cara's house and parks in the driveway. "At least we know she's home on a Monday morning."

"Which means she either works a later shift or works from home," I say, unclicking my seat belt.

"Let's find out." Nolan gets out of the car, and I do the same.

We only make it about two steps before a patrol car blocks us in the driveway. Nolan and I exchange a look.

Detective Lange gets out of the patrol car. "I thought I saw you following me."

Busted. And here I'd thought we were careful about keeping our distance. Maybe Detective Lange wasn't pausing to answer a call. Maybe he paused because he caught sight of us in his rearview mirror.

I know it's stupid, but I can't stop myself from saying, "I noticed you were using your phone without handsfree while driving. I do believe that's against the law, Detective."

"You know what else is against the law? Tampering with a police investigation."

"Who's doing that?" Nolan asks.

Detective Lange steps toward us. "Don't play dumb."

"What's dumb is thinking we're in any way impeding your investigation. We offered to help you, but you're too stubborn to admit you need help from anyone." Nolan's face is turning bright red.

I close the distance between us and take his hand in mine, hoping to calm him a bit.

"I think you might change your perspective after spending some time in a holding cell down at the station," Detective Lange says.

"What?" I shriek.

"What could you possibly have to throw us in jail for?" Nolan asks.

"How about for stalking an officer of the law?" Detective Lange smirks, and it takes all my might not to smack the stupid expression right off his face.

"Maybe investigating Donna Barrett is making you act like her," I say. "You're paranoid and thinking everyone is watching you. We told you we wanted to talk to Cara Romney. Whether or not you're here is beside the point."

"Tell it to the judge," Detective Lange says. "Both of you in the back of the patrol car before I slap handcuffs on you, too."

"This is completely absurd," Nolan spits out.

"I don't really care what you think about it." Detective Lange opens the back door of the patrol car. "Get in before I charge you with resisting arrest as well."

No matter how bogus these charges are, we don't have a choice but to cooperate. We're going to jail.

Chapter Ten

On the drive to the station, I take out my phone to call Autumn. I need to let her know what happened.

"No phone calls," Detective Lange says, glaring at me through the rearview mirror.

"I believe I'm entitled to one by law," I say.

"You will be after you're booked. Now put the phone away before I pull over and confiscate it."

I shove the phone back into my pocket. I should keep my mouth shut, but at this point I'm going to jail anyway, so why not speak my mind? "You know what your problem is?"

"That I don't have a muzzle to keep you quiet?" Detective Lange asks.

"Funny but incorrect. Your problem is that you're so selfish you can't see the big picture."

"I'm selfish?" He scoffs.

"Yes. It's a classic case of older sibling resenting the baby of the family."

"Here we go. You're going to spout some psychobabble about how I wanted to be an only child, and it's unfair to poor Nolan, who got everything he ever wanted and more."

"No, he didn't. He got a jerk for an older brother. I'm sure that's not what he wanted by any means."

"Yeah, well then neither one of us got what we wanted." Detective Lange starts playing music to drown me out.

I lean back in the seat and cross my arms, completely done with Detective Lange and his nonsense.

The station is pretty empty when we arrive. Detective Lange brings us to a holding cell. "Inside," he says.

"You haven't read us our rights or anything," Nolan says.

"I haven't decided what to do with you yet, so I'm giving you time to think about your actions and consider what to do from here. You're welcome."

"Don't act like you're doing us any favors," Nolan says as Detective Lange closes the door on us.

He doesn't get a response. Detective Lange turns and walks away.

"I can't believe this," Nolan says, sitting on the small bench in the cell.

I turn to smile at him.

"What can you possibly be smiling about?" he asks.

"Oh, just the fact that since we weren't booked and processed, we still have our phones."

"Calling Autumn isn't going to help," he says, looking down at the floor.

"No, but calling Annabelle might." I sit down next to him. "You know she wants you two to work things out. If you call her and tell her Drew locked us up, she'll either call to scream at him or come down here in person."

Nolan meets my gaze. "I'm hoping for coming here in person. I want him to be humiliated in front of his colleagues when his wife reams him out."

"Make the call," I say.

He pulls his phone from his pocket and dials, putting the phone to his ear. "Annabelle, it's Nolan. Look, I'm not sure what's going on, but Drew threw Sydney and me in a holding cell at the station a few minutes ago."

I can't make out the exact words she's saying, but the high-pitched shrill of her voice reaches my ears. She's clearly not happy with her husband.

"Would you be willing to come to the station and talk to him. He won't listen to reason, but I think he'll listen to you."

More loud shrieks from her end.

"Thanks, Annabelle. We appreciate it." Nolan ends the call and pockets his phone again. "Now we wait."

I'm guessing Annabelle breaks a few laws on her way to the station because she makes it in record time. All we can hear down here is commotion upstairs, but I'm certain it's Annabelle. Then there are two sets of footsteps on the stairs.

Annabelle is leading the way, which I admit I find amusing. She's totally letting Drew know she's in charge even if this is his job. I really do like this woman. As soon as she spots us in the cell she rushes over to us. "Are you okay?"

"We're fine," Nolan tells her, getting up to join her at the bars, and I do the same.

"Drew Lange, you let them out of that holding cell this instant," Annabelle says, turning to face her husband. "That man is your brother. I can't believe you'd turn your back on family like that. All these years, I thought you'd been shortchanged. I sided with you. But now you have the opportunity to make up for lost time and fix what your parents took away from both of you, and what do you do?" She throws out one hand, motioning to us. "You lock up Nolan. This is unacceptable. I didn't marry a man callous enough to not see Nolan was hurt by your parents just as much as you were."

I have to hand it to Annabelle. She'd make a pretty good psychologist with the way she analyzed their relationship. Of course, yelling at patients is frowned upon.

"This has nothing to do with our personal relationship. They were following me and disrupting my investigation. I would have done the same to anyone else." He crosses his arms. "Actually, I did them a favor because I haven't charged them with anything yet. I'm simply forcing them to cool off and think about how wrong their actions were."

Annabelle's voice gets lower, and she speaks so slowly I get chills down my spine. "I'm not going to repeat myself, Drew."

"Sweetheart, you don't understand."

"What I understand is that you are not the man I married. So ask yourself if you'd like to sleep in the cell next to them tonight because I refuse to let this person"—she gestures to him, her hand rising and falling from his head to his feet—"into my home."

Detective Lange's nostrils flare, and he's clenching his jaw as he reaches for the keys in his pocket. He unlocks the door to the cell.

Nolan and I don't waste any time in stepping out.

"Thank you," I say to Annabelle.

"Let me apologize for my husband. That's twice now I've had to do that." She turns to Drew. "And let me be very clear that I don't plan to make this a habit. Either get your act together and act like the man I fell in love with, or you can pack your bags, Drew Lange." She turns on her heel and marches back up the stairs.

"Get out of my sight," Detective Lange says to us.

Nolan and I hurry up the stairs. I have no doubt Drew is going to break down and cry after that, and I don't want to be here when he does. I'm pretty sure me witnessing him at his weakest would ruin any hope of him even tolerating me in the future.

We walk out of the station, and Nolan calls a cab for us since his car is still at Cara Romney's house. We're both quiet on the way. The cab driver pulls up to Cara's house.

"My car is gone," Nolan says.

"How?" I ask.

"She must have had it towed."

Of course, she did because Detective Lange neglected to tell her why Nolan's car was left parked in her driveway. She didn't even know who the car belonged to.

"If it was towed," the cab driver says, "you'll need to pick it up at the tow yard. You want me to bring you there?"

"Yes. Thank you," Nolan says. "This day keeps getting worse."

I don't bother telling him the jail cell was definitely the low point of the day. All he has to do is pay a fee and show proof of ownership of the car, and he'll get his vehicle back. The day has practically been a wash as far as the case goes, though. We never got to question Cara Romney.

"I want this day to be over," Nolan says.

"I know what you mean. Let's get your car and go back to my place." There's a huge part of me that doesn't want to look into the case anymore. Detective Lange doesn't want us to help him find the killer, so why are we trying so hard?

"I hope you have wine. I really need a glass or three."

After picking up Nolan's car, we drive to my place. Luckily, I had a lasagna prepped in the fridge, so I stick it in the oven and prepare some garlic bread and a Caesar salad. Nolan pours the wine, which is red, not my favorite, but I'm willing to drink anything right now to take the edge off. I sip it and take a seat at the center island.

"If it weren't for you, I'd think I made a huge mistake moving back to Swan Creek," Nolan says, picking a crouton off the salad and popping it into his mouth.

I grab two bowls and scoop salad into each for us. "I give you a lot of credit for coming back here."

"Why? If you ask Drew, my life was a cake walk."

"Your brother likes to feel sorry for himself because he thinks if he doesn't, no one else will." I sip my wine before forking some salad into my mouth.

"You think so?"

I nod. "He didn't get the attention he wanted from your parents, so he went into a profession where he'd get acknowledgment and credit for everything he does."

"I guess you're right. I'm surprised he didn't become a reporter so he could get bylines on everything."

I bob one shoulder. "It's possible he thinks that's why you became a reporter."

Nolan wipes his mouth with a napkin. "That's not why I became a reporter."

I reach for his hand, placing mine on top of it. "I know that. But what I'm learning from this case is that people tend to interpret the things around them in ways that make sense to them, not necessarily how things really are. Like how Donna thought Neil Thatcher was stalking her when really he was only doing his job."

"Why do you think Donna was so paranoid?"

"I'm not sure. She never mentioned any childhood issues like…" I let the rest of my sentence trail off.

"Like my brother and I have?" He looks down at his salad. "It's okay. You can say it."

"The problem is she withheld too much from me. After dinner, I'm going to dive into my notes again and see if I can find any hint of emotional trauma that might have led to this behavior.

I'm still awake at one in the morning. Nolan left around eleven after deciding a good night's sleep would do him more good than several glasses of wine to drown his sorrows in. I think he made the right call there. I've been pouring over my notes for the past two hours, and just now, I come across something that might be important.

"Theater parents are the worst. They're never home and they have creepy costumes in their closets."

"Do you know someone who had parents who worked in the theater?" I ask since this seems to be a topic that holds importance to her.

She waves off my comment. "I'm just making an observation. I'm a people watcher. You can tell a lot about a person by observing them."

I remember this session. It was when she first started coming to see me. I thought she was testing me, trying to see if that was my process: observing people to analyze their behaviors. The comment about theater parents was quickly washed over and never brought up again. What if her own parents worked in the theater? That would explain her aversion to costumes. Maybe it wasn't so much a fear as a hatred for them. That could also explain how she ended up at the haunted house. A true fear of costumes would have prevented her from going. But a hatred for costumes might not, especially since she was wearing one as well.

It's possible I wasn't all that far off the mark when I told Detective Lange that working Donna Barrett's case was making him paranoid like she was. Maybe the truth of the matter is that they're both alike to begin with because of the impact their parents had on their lives. Donna resented their lack of presence in her life. Just like Drew does. What if the hole that created in her is what led to her not being able to form solid relationships with other people? She jumped on the marriage band wagon and pressured Pierce. Is that because she was determined to find someone who would be a constant in her life the way her parents failed to be?

As much as I hate to admit it, I think Drew Lange is actually helping me figure out who Donna Barrett really was.

Chapter Eleven

I make sure to be there for all of my Tuesday appointments since I've had to cancel on so many clients recently. They've been really understanding since they know about Donna's death and that she was one of my patients. I'm thankful to have such great people to work with.

By the time Billy Danvers comes into my office, I'm emotionally taxed. Thomas Moss, my patient with high anxiety, put me through the ringer. His incessant gum popping is getting out of control. I really do need to consider instituting the no gum chewing rule I've contemplated in the past. The sound grates on my nerves, today more than usual.

Billy flops down in the bean bag chair like usual. "Hey, Doc."

"How are you today, Billy?"

"I'm worried about graduating in the spring."

Billy is homeschooled. He used to go to public school, but he got bullied so much his parents pulled him out. He's a great kid. He just had the unfortunate luck of being emotional around the wrong kids in school.

"What about it has you worried?" I ask, sitting down in the arm chair beside the bean bag.

"I have to find a job."

"Well, that can be exciting. Have you given any thought to what you'd like to do?"

He shrugs and pulls at a string on the hem of his black hoodie. "I'm good with computers, but who isn't these days?"

"Do you mean coding?"

He rolls his eyes. "My six-year-old cousin can code. I'm good at fixing computer problems."

"Like technical support?" I ask.

"I guess so."

"Have you considered applying for jobs in tech support with companies that sell computers and such?"

"You mean like those people who drive out to other people's houses to fix their computers?"

"Possibly if that would be of interest to you."

"I definitely don't want a desk job, and that would allow me to get a change of scenery." He pauses, and I know he's weighing the pros and cons of the job. "Maybe. I'll look into it later when I'm home."

"Good. So that means you have a potential plan for after you graduate, and it's only October. I'd say you're ahead of the game."

After our session ends, I check in with Lena at the front desk.

"You look exhausted," she says.

"I feel exhausted."

"Well, I have potentially good news then. Your appointment right after lunch has to reschedule. Flu season seems to be hitting hard this year."

"Sorry to hear that, but I guess it means extra-long lunch breaks for you and me."

"Why do I get the feeling your lunch break won't involve much of a break at all?" she asks, giving me a slightly reprimanding look.

"Because you know me so well." I tap my hand against her desk before walking out of the office. Nolan and I are meeting Autumn and Aaron at the youth center. Autumn's having lunch delivered from the pizza place down the road. They make incredible baked ziti and garlic knots. My stomach rumbles at the thought.

I wind up beating Nolan there, and I go inside to find Autumn. She's in the lunch room, which really is more of a conference room, but it's where the kids eat. The food smells incredible, and I get to work helping her uncover everything and put out the plates and silverware.

"I hope you don't mind, but I invited Kevin. It seemed awkward not to since he's living here now," she tells me.

"No problem." I want to talk to him anyway.

"I got the drinks," Aaron says, walking in with a two-liter bottle of ginger ale and what appears to be a gallon of iced tea.

"Thanks, hon," Autumn says. "Where's Nolan?" she asks me.

"Not sure. I haven't talked to him yet this morning."

As if on cue, Nolan walks into the room.

"Speak of the devil," Autumn says.

"I'm a devil now? I think you might be confusing me with my brother." His joke comes off as sad more than amusing.

I walk over to him and kiss him lightly on the lips. I don't need to say anything. He knows I picked up on how he's feeling about Drew right now.

We all take our seats and dig in. Kevin arrives before we start eating.

"Sorry I'm late," he says. "I wanted to finish up with that paperwork you gave me."

"First rule if you're going to work here," Aaron says. "No work is more important than lunch." He winks at Kevin, who smiles back at him.

"Got it. I like that rule."

"Kevin, do you mind telling us about how Donna Barrett got you fired from the laundromat." I'm interested in hearing his side of the story because I'm thinking Donna's perspective on life was less than accurate.

Kevin looks at Autumn, who gives him an encouraging nod. "I had just washed the floors. I do it every morning." He pauses and then corrects himself. "I *did* it every morning. The morning regulars knew to be careful. Donna wasn't a morning regular though. She was getting some dry cleaning done."

"And she slipped on the wet floor?" Nolan asks between bites of his baked ziti.

Kevin nods. "She fell, but she didn't get hurt or anything. At least, I don't see how she could have. She caught the counter on the way down, so she stopped her momentum before she hit the floor. She claimed she sprained her ankle, though. And she blamed me."

"She stopped herself from falling?" I ask.

He nods. "The wet floor sign was up. I swear. She just didn't see it. Everyone else did, though. You can ask them."

"We believe you, Kevin. Donna had some issues with blaming people for things that weren't really their fault," I say.

"What do you mean, Syd?" Autumn asks.

I'm not thrilled to talk about the case in front of Kevin, but it seems like he's a pretty permanent fixture around here now. I don't really see another option. "In every situation, Donna felt like the victim. Take Pierce Crawford for example. She was pressuring him to marry her, yet in her mind, he was the bully in the relationship because he wouldn't propose."

"She twisted the situation so the blame was on him," Aaron says.

"Exactly. Then there was Neil Thatcher. She got a restraining order against him for stalking her at the food store, but according to Neil, he was doing his job stocking shelves. I think Donna was going to the aisles where she saw Neil because she felt the need to keep an eye on him, but really she was making it so he was always there."

"Neil wouldn't hurt a fly," Kevin says. "He's so shy. He doesn't even like when people make direct eye contact with him."

Hmm, if Donna made direct eye contact and Neil kept looking away, she might have thought that seemed suspicious, like he was trying to avoid being caught staring at her.

"Wait, do you think she knew she was lying about all of it? Was she manipulating the situations on purpose to make herself be the victim?" Autumn asks.

I shake my head. "I don't think so. I think it's all about perception. In her mind, she believed she was being stalked, but in reality, she was placing herself in his presence. And she was probably making him act strangely because she kept looking at him."

"That's pretty crazy." Nolan taps his chin. "She might have caused the whole incident herself."

"It would make sense that's what happened," I say.

"How do you explain the sign at the laundromat?" Kevin asks me before shoving an entire garlic knot into his mouth.

That I haven't figured out yet. "Where was the sign?"

"At the counter where the wet floor was. She was standing right by it."

"Was she carrying her dry cleaning?"

Kevin furrows his brow like he's trying to remember. "I don't know. Maybe? I don't remember if she was dropping off or picking up her dry cleaning at the time."

I think back to what I read in my notes last night. "Donna told me she liked to watch people and analyze their behavior."

"Sounds like she was trying to create a common ground with you," Aaron says.

"Maybe. Or she really was a people watcher. That explains Neil being uncomfortable and acting strangely when she was shopping in the same aisles where he was stocking shelves. And it also means that Donna might have been so busy looking around at the people inside the laundromat that she didn't even notice the sign."

Kevin points his fork in my direction. "Because the sign was on the floor, below her level of sight if she was watching the other people in the laundromat. That's good."

"What about the neighbor?" Nolan asks. "Do you think that was a normal feud between neighbors, or did Donna somehow blow that out of proportion, too?

"I don't know about that one. I'll need to look closer at my notes and talk to the neighbor myself."

"We still need to talk to Cara Romney. I called her this morning and set up a meeting for six after you're done with your sessions for the day."

"I have a break right after lunch because one of my patients is sick with the flu. Think Cara will see us then instead?"

"I'll call her now and find out." He stands up and walks out of the lunch room to make the call.

"Hey, Doc, I want to thank you for your help with that cop. Getting him off my back and all." Kevin looks down at his plate. "It must not be a comfortable situation seeing as he's your boyfriend's brother."

"Don't worry about me. I'm just glad you're doing well."

He gestures to Autumn and Aaron. "Thanks to these two. They've done more for me than all the other people in my life combined."

Autumn wipes a tear from her eye. "I told you, Kevin. We're a family here. No one messes with my family."

Nolan returns. "We're all set, Syd. Cara works from home, so she doesn't care what time we come by." He smirks. "Her only request was that we don't let a certain police detective tag along with us."

"I take it she didn't care for Drew." I can't help smiling.

"Not at all. I'm guessing he knew we were following him, and it made him extra cranky when he was interrogating her."

Sounds like Drew.

"You can leave your car here, Syd, if you two want to ride together. We're still officially closed since Detective Lange hasn't solved the case yet."

I know they're all eager to get the youth center open again. Those kids need this place. "Nolan and I are working as fast as we can to figure out who killed Donna Barrett."

Autumn reaches for my hand. "I know you are."

Cara Romney answers the door in a cream pants suit. Pretty fancy attire for someone who works at home.

"Ms. Romney?" Nolan asks.

"Yes. I suppose you're Mr. Lange and Doctor Warner."

"You can call us Nolan and Sydney," I say.

She nods. "Please, come in." She steps aside to let us in.

Her demeanor, dress, and the expensive furnishings in her house don't mesh with the impression I had of her from what Donna and Pierce told me. I was expecting a social butterfly who cared more about partying than working.

"Ms. Romney, can I ask what you do for a living?" I say as she leads us to the living room.

"I'm a psychiatrist. I mostly work with people who don't leave their homes. You know over video calls, but some of my clients do come here for sessions."

I stop walking and look at Nolan. He's clearly thinking the same thing I am. If Donna's best friend was a psychiatrist, why would Donna pay to see me?

"Is something wrong?" she asks, taking a seat in an arm chair.

Nolan and I recover and sit down on the black leather couch. "I'm sorry; it's just that I'm a little surprised Donna didn't come to you for therapy instead of me."

"Oh, she did."

Oh my goodness! The truth of the situation hits me hard. Donna and Cara weren't best friends. That's just how Donna perceived their relationship. "You and Donna had a patient-client relationship then," I say, cluing Nolan in on what I realized.

"Wait," Nolan says. "I was under the impression that you and Donna were friends."

"Donna was an extremely disturbed woman. I saw her just about every day of the week."

Which is how Donna convinced Pierce that Cara was her best friend. I can see how he'd be fooled when Donna was always talking about being with Cara. She failed to mention she was seeing her for therapy.

"Was Donna on any medications?" I ask since that's Cara's area of expertise and not mine.

"She refused medication. That's when I suggested she start seeing a psychologist instead."

Was Cara trying to get rid of Donna as a client? Passing her off on me?

"I'm assuming you told Detective Lange this," Nolan says.

"Yes, he's aware of my diagnosis of Donna's condition."

I'm going to assume that diagnosis was that Donna suffered from schizophrenia. "I apologize for calling you Ms. Romney, Doctor."

She waves a hand in the air. "It doesn't bother me in the least." Yet she was careful to address me as doctor when we arrived.

"Doctor, in your opinion, was Donna dangerous?"

"She was quite delusional. She thought everyone in her life was out to get her in some way, but she was also very good at fooling people. Do you know it took me three years to figure out she was schizophrenic? She could hide it quite well."

"I know exactly what you mean. I've been seeing Donna for about a year and a half, and while I knew she had some issues, I did not suspect schizophrenia."

Cara laces her hands in her lap.

Something is still bothering me. "Pierce Crawford, Donna's ex-boyfriend, said they were at a party with you a little while back."

"Donna thought she was attending the party with me. The truth is she crashed it. I let it slide because I figured confronting her in front of everyone, including her boyfriend, would not end well."

I agree. "You were convincing as Donna's friend. Pierce believed it."

"I'm sure he did."

"According to Donna, she went to the haunted house with you."

"That's not exactly how it happened. She called me, saying she dressed up and went to the haunted house but was totally freaking out. She begged me to come help her."

"Did you?" I ask.

Doctor Romney's body language gives her away. She went to the haunted house, and something happened that she doesn't want to admit to.

"What happened between you two at the youth center that night?" I ask.

"I think it's time you both leave." She stands up.

"You'd had enough of her by then, hadn't you?" I ask, standing up as well.

Nolan joins me, looking very concerned by where I'm going with my questioning.

"That's why you didn't want us bringing Detective Lange along. He didn't figure out that you went to the haunted house. He probably only asked if you invited Donna there, and you could honestly answer no to that."

"Sydney," Nolan says, tugging on my arm. "Let's go. She wants us to leave."

"Yes, leave now, or I'm calling the police."

"Go ahead and call," I say, crossing my arms.

"Syd." Nolan's voice is louder and sterner than before.

"Make the call, Doctor. I think the police should know you were there that night and that you fought with Donna. The question is did you fight to the point of sticking a knife into her chest?"

Chapter Twelve

Cara Romney's composure falters for a split second. Then she grabs her phone from the pocket of her dress pants and dials. "This is Doctor Cara Romney. There are two trespassers in my home who refuse to leave. Please come immediately." She rattles off her address before hanging up.

I sit back down on the couch and cross my arms. I'm not leaving until the police know the truth. "It was probably easy for you to fool Detective Lange, huh? You just carefully answered the questions you wanted to answer. If I had to guess, I'd say you made him believe Donna was delusional. You probably told him she made up your friendship entirely. The fact that you weren't at the haunted house when the body was found must have made him drop that line of questioning completely."

She sits back down and stares at me but doesn't say a word. She's going to keep an eye on us until the police get here.

Nolan whips his phone out of his pocket. "I'm calling Drew." He brings the phone to his ear. "It's Nolan. Are you on your way to Cara Romney's house?" He pauses. "Yeah, it's us, but the real reason she called the cops is—" He pulls the phone away from his ear and looks at the screen. "He hung up on me."

Cara Romney laughs. "This is going to be easier than I thought."

I didn't stop to consider that Drew would gladly lock us up again. He'd have a valid reason to this time since Cara is going to press charges for trespassing. "How do you live with it?" I ask her. "You went into this profession to help people. How can you sit there so smugly knowing you lied to the police? That you blew up at a patient? That you resorted to murder?"

"I didn't kill her."

"Then tell us what really did happen," I say.

"I don't owe you an explanation."

"Donna was one of my patients. I have a right to know what happened to her."

"She brought this on herself. Don't think she didn't come to me complaining about you."

My head jerks back like I was sucker punched. "She complained about me to you?"

"Of course. Who didn't the woman complain about?"

"What did she say?" I don't know why I want to know, especially since it's clear Donna had a lot of issues and made up things all the time.

"She said you didn't really listen. You only pretended to. And she told me it was your idea she go to the haunted house."

"She told me you pressured her to go," I say. "I never told her to go. I told her dressing up as Greta Garbo might be a good first step to get over her fear of costumes and later Halloween in general, but I told her to think about doing that next year. I didn't push her, and I never told her to go to the haunted house. That was too much for her."

"Clearly. But she went, didn't she?"

"Did you ever talk to her about going?" I ask.

Cara shakes her head. "I mentioned some of my friends were going."

And Donna probably saw that as an invitation since she thought she was best friends with Cara. "What exactly did she say when she called you from the haunted house?"

"She was crying. She said she'd taken your advice and dressed up. That she went to the haunted house and she was scared out of her mind."

"So you went to help her?" I ask.

"I know how she is. I figured I'd call her a cab and it would be over, but when I got there, she insisted it was my fault she was in the situation in the first place."

Donna couldn't keep her lies straight. She told Cara I encouraged her to go to the haunted house, and she told me it was Cara who did so. But she got confused at the haunted house because she was so frightened. She probably forgot whom she said what to.

"What happened after that?" Nolan asks.

"I offered to call her a cab, but she refused to leave."

"Why?" I ask.

Cara shrugs. "I can't really say. I told her if she wasn't going to let me help her, I was leaving. And I did."

"The verbal altercation, did it get loud?"

"Our voices were raised, mostly Donna's. But it was so dark I'm not sure anyone would know who it was they were hearing."

The doorbell rings, making us all jump. I'd almost forgotten we were waiting for the police. Cara gets up to answer the door.

"What do you think?" Nolan asks me once we're alone.

"I'm not sure. This is a lot to take in all at once."

When Cara returns to the living room, Drew is with her. "Let's go," he says to us.

"Detective," Cara says, "as long as they leave with you now, I won't press charges."

I can't believe she's going to pretend like our conversation never happened. "We'll leave," I say, "right after you tell Detective Lange what you told us."

Drew looks at Cara. "Is there something I should know?"

"Doctor to doctor, you can't keep this to yourself. I get that you think it paints you in a bad light, but the truth is going to come out, and how do you think it's going to look if you withhold this information now? Detective Lange will come back and haul you to the station as a suspect."

"Everyone, sit," Drew bellows.

Cara sighs. "Fine." She dives into an abbreviated version of last Friday night.

"Let me get this straight," Drew says. "You lied about being at the haunted house."

"No. I did no such thing. You never asked me if I was there."

Just like I suspected. She threw him off by telling him about her diagnosis of Donna's condition.

"I answered every one of your questions honestly, Detective."

"What time did you leave?" he asks her.

"I didn't look at the time, so I can't say for sure."

"Where was Donna when you left her?" he asks, his jaw clenched.

"It was dark, Detective. I never intended to go to the haunted house, so I can't say where we were exactly."

Something Kevin told us when Drew questioned him hits me like a ton a bricks. "Wait a second. Someone saw you with Donna that night."

"So? The place was packed."

"Yes, this person didn't know who you were. He only said you were in costume. A white flapper-style dress."

Cara's face loses all color. "I—"

"Why would you be in costume if you only went to the haunted house because Cara called you in a panic?" I ask.

Cara looks down at the ground. "I want a lawyer."

"Does this mean it's over?" Autumn asks. She invited Nolan and me over for dinner.

"Usually, people only lawyer up when they're guilty and don't want to incriminate themselves," Nolan says. "I haven't spoken to Drew, but he seemed pretty sure he'd found the killer when he took Cara out of her house and escorted her to the police station."

"It was what Kevin told us that led to everything unraveling. Cara tried to tell us she didn't go to the haunted house with Donna, but Kevin remembered the woman with Donna was in costume."

"Ah," Aaron says. "That's definitely a detail that gives away what really happened."

"So it's a case of a psychiatrist snapping on a particularly trying patient." Autumn tsks and shakes her head.

"I still feel so stupid for not picking up on the fact that Donna was schizophrenic. I should have seen the signs, but people with problems like that usually sees psychiatrists so they can get medical help for their condition." I don't prescribe medications. I talk people through their troubles.

Nolan reaches for my hand and squeezes it. "Even Cara said she was fooled for years. You can't blame yourself."

"Yeah, seriously, Syd. Look how many people Donna Barrett fooled." Autumn raises her glass of wine to her lips.

I know they're right, but I thought my degree would have allowed me to see what others couldn't.

"I'm just glad this means the youth center can reopen," Autumn says.

"We still have to wait for the okay from Detective Lange," Aaron says.

Autumn rolls her eyes, and I know she's biting her tongue to keep from giving her opinion of Detective Lange in front of Nolan.

"You know, we didn't even get to finish looking into all our suspects this time," Nolan says.

"Isn't that the point?" Aaron asks. "You only look until you find the guilty party. After that, what's left to do?" He stands up and starts clearing the empty plates.

I get up and help Autumn load the dishwasher.

"What's really bugging you?" she asks me, taking a rinsed plate from my hand and loading it into the bottom rack of the dishwasher.

"I don't know. Something feels off about this whole case."

"Well, yeah. Cara Romney lost it and killed one of her own clients."

The whole story about Cara going to the haunted house to help Donna didn't make any sense from the start because she wouldn't have brought a knife with her if her intention was to call a cab for Donna. No. The entire thing was premeditated. It makes sense that Cara convinced Donna to go, and they both dressed up in costume. The costume probably allowed Cara to conceal the knife she'd brought with her. And she most likely wore gloves with her flapper dress. It all adds up, and that's the problem.

Donna's perspective was almost never correct. If she told me Cara was trying to get her to go to the haunted house, then that can't be what actually happened.

As soon as the dishes are taken care of, I turn to Autumn. "I'm going to call it an early night."

"But we haven't even had dessert yet. I bought a marble cheese-cake just for you."

"That's sweet of you, but there's something I need to do."

"At eight o'clock at night?" Nolan asks, walking up behind me. "What's going on, Syd?"

"I need to go through my notes from my last session with Donna again. There's something I'm missing."

"The police already have Cara Romney in custody," Aaron says. "You have to let this go, Sydney."

"I can't. Something's wrong. The answer has to be in my session notes, and I need to find it before the wrong woman ends up behind bars."

"Are you saying you're convinced Cara Romney isn't the killer?" Nolan asks.

Convinced is a strong word. I'm not convinced of anything. "I need to be sure." We drove here separately, so I step toward Nolan and kiss him goodnight. "Stay. Eat a slice of cheesecake for me."

"No. I'm going to come with you," he says.

I shake my head. "I'll be more focused if you aren't there."

"Are you saying I'm distracting?" Nolan asks, looking slightly offended.

"Easy there," Autumn says. "I think it's actually a compliment."

"It is," I assure him. "I'll call you later."

I race out of there, in a hurry to sit down with my notes and find out what I'm missing.

I pour over the notes countless times. At one point, I drift off to sleep, sitting up in bed with the notebook on my lap. When I wake up in the morning, my body is screaming at me for the awkward position I stayed in all night.

"Ow, ow, ow," I say aloud even though I live alone. I look around the empty bedroom. "I really need a dog."

I pick up the notebook, ready to toss it aside when my gaze lands on a name. "Bentley. Donna had a dog. What happened to the dog?" I ask the air.

I grab the phone from my nightstand and call the last person I ever thought I'd call in a moment of need.

"Detective Lange," he answers.

"Drew, it's Sydney."

"What do you want? The case is over."

"I'm assuming some officers went to Donna Barrett's house after she died."

"She didn't have a next of kin. The house went to the bank."

"So no one went to get Donna's dog?" That poor creature.

"She had a dog?" he asks.

"Yes! You need to go get it."

I hear him typing away on his computer. "There's no record of a dog license with Donna's name attached to it."

Whether or not she got a license for her dog isn't really my concern at the moment. "You need to go to her house."

"Sydney, the bank has already been there to lock it up. They do a walk through. If they'd found a dog, they would have notified me."

"What are you saying?"

"She didn't have a dog."

"Then who is Bentley?" I ask.

"Probably a figment of her imagination."

From everything I know about Donna, I'm willing to bet Bentley is someone or something in her life. And I have a feeling I need to find him fast.

Chapter Thirteen

Getting through my morning appointments isn't easy because the only thing I can focus on is talking to Cara Romney to find out if she knows who or what Bentley is. A car? A pet of some nature? A person? I don't know. But Donna mentioned him to me in our last session in connection to Halloween. She talked about dressing him up as a spider. Maybe it doesn't mean anything, but my gut is telling me to look into it.

Once it's lunchtime, I tell Lena I'll be running out and might be a few minutes late getting back for my first afternoon appointment.

"No problem. I'll hold down the fort in your absence."

I rush out and drive to the police station. Detective Lange is at his desk. He looks up at me but keeps typing away on his computer.

"Detective, I'd like to speak to Cara Romney."

"What for?"

"She knew Donna Barrett better than anyone. I need to find out who Bentley really is."

"This is a waste of time, Sydney."

"Why? Did you get Cara Romney to confess to the murder?"

He shakes his head. "Not yet, but she will."

"What is she saying?" I sit down in the seat opposite his even though he hasn't invited me to.

"I'm not going to tell you that, and you know it."

"Fine. It doesn't matter. I just need to talk to Cara."

"I see no good reason to let you back there."

"That means she's still here. You haven't got enough to charge her, do you?"

He shifts in his seat, which is all the answer I need.

"What are you going to do when your twenty-four hours are up and you can't legally hold her?"

He doesn't respond.

"You can't possibly be so stubborn that you'd let a suspect go because you won't take help from me."

He stands up. "Follow me, but understand I'm leading this line of questioning."

That's impossible. He doesn't even know what to ask, but I need him to bring me to Cara Romney, so I hold up both hands in front of me as if I'm surrendering to what he said.

He walks me downstairs. Because he can't actually charge Cara with murder yet, he has her in a room instead of a holding cell. Of course, it's the only room on the same floor as the holding cells. I'm sure his plan was to walk her by the cells in an attempt to show her what is in store for her in the future. I'm also sure Cara figured that out for herself and wasn't intimidated by the move.

He closes the door behind us. "Dr. Romney, we have a few more questions for you."

"I'm assuming you called my lawyer then, and he's on his way." She leans back in her seat and pretends to inspect her fingernails.

"I have a question that actually has nothing to do with you," I say, earning me a scathing glare from Drew.

Cara raises her gaze to me. "You can ask. I won't say I'll answer, but go ahead and give it a whirl."

"Who's Bentley?"

Cara's reaction confuses me. She stiffens but looks really confused at the same time.

"Clearly the name means something to you. Donna told me that was the name of her dog, but there's no record of her having a dog."

Cara shakes her head. "Bentley isn't a dog. I can't believe she told you that." The very idea seems to upset her.

"Cara, who is he then?" I ask, taking the seat across from her. I'm hoping calling her by her first name will make her feel more at ease with me. "Please. You have to help me figure this out. It's the only way to get you out of here."

"Hold on," Drew says. "No one is getting out of here unless I say so."

"Or your twenty-four hours are up," Cara and I say at the same time.

"I'm putting an end to this," Drew says. "Sydney, let's go." He opens the door.

"Bentley Schlater is one of my patients," Cara says, making Detective Lange pause. She looks directly at me. "I see him every day right before Donna. That must be how they met. They'd cross paths when he was leaving and she'd be waiting to see me."

"What does he see you for?" I ask.

"You know I can't tell you that. I shouldn't have to explain doctor-patient confidentiality to you."

"Fine. I'll find him and figure it out myself." I stand up.

"That's it? You're leaving me here with him?" she asks.

"If you have nothing further to say to me, I'm finished here." I know I'm putting her in an impossible situation, but I can't help her if she's not going to give a little.

She groans. "All I can tell you is that Bentley is a small man."

"Cute?" I ask, remembering Donna's description of him.

"Some might say that, yes."

"Why would Donna talk about dressing him up as a spider?" I ask.

"He has a pet spider. I don't think Donna would like that, but she never discussed it with me. She never even told me she and Bentley had become friends."

Yet Donna saw him as a pet of sorts. "What do you make of her telling me Bentley was her dog?" I ask.

She shrugs. "He's fiercely loyal. That's a quality many pet owners look for in their dogs."

Loyalty would be important to Donna. Maybe Bentley was the only one to take what she said at face value without questioning her. "Is there any chance Bentley is the type to stalk someone?"

She leans forward, resting her arms on the table in front of her. "Are you asking me if I think Bentley is capable of stalking and murdering Donna Barrett?"

We're clearly all wondering about it right now.

Drew closes the door and sits down. "Doctor Romney, I need you to answer my questions. If this Bentley Schlater could be a suspect, you can't withhold evidence, or I'll charge you with obstruction. And I will make that charge stick. I can assure you of that."

"This is different, Detective. Bentley isn't dead. I can't hand over his files to you."

"Then I'll get a warrant. Or better yet, I'll call Bentley into the station."

"He won't handle that well. Not at all. He'll need me with him."

Drew stands up. "Yeah, well that's not going to happen seeing as you're still at the top of my suspect list. Sit tight, Doc." He taps the table twice before moving for the door. "Sydney, let's go."

"Dr. Warner," Cara says, "please make sure you're there. Tell Bentley I sent you. That might make him feel a little better."

I'm not sure Drew will allow it, but Cara looks really worried about her patient, and I have to sympathize with her there. "I'll do what I can," I tell her before following Drew out of the room.

As we walk back upstairs, he says, "You know I can't allow it."

"Do you want Bentley to freak out and not cooperate with you? You don't know what you might be dealing with. Having me there is in everyone's best interest."

"You can't keep weaseling your way into my interrogations."

"If Donna was drawn to Bentley, he was probably worse off than she was. She was schizophrenic. Do you know how to handle someone with an illness like that, Detective?"

He sits down at his desk. "I'm calling Bentley Schlater in now. You sit."

I do as he says, happy he didn't tell me to leave. This means he's at least considering letting me stay while he questions Bentley.

I don't say a word as he looks up Bentley's number and makes the phone call. When he's finished dialing, I whisper, "Tell him Cara is here, and we need him to come down to the station."

He covers the receiver. "I'm not letting him see Cara." He quickly removes his hand. "Is this Mr. Schlater? Bentley Schlater?"

I can't hear Bentley on the other end.

"This is Detective Andrew Lange with the Swan Creek Police Department."

Another pause.

"I'm going to need you to come down to the station so I can talk to you."

Now I do hear Bentley. He's upset.

Detective Lange covers the receiver. "He thinks this is about some gum he stole when he was six," he whispers to me.

"Give me the phone."

"No," he whisper yells.

"Give me the phone," I insist, thrusting my hand out.

He groans but hands me the phone.

Bentley is crying now.

"Bentley? Bentley this is Dr. Sydney Warner. I'm a friend of Dr. Romney's."

"You know Doc Romney?" he asks, sniffling.

"Yes. She's here, too. We'd like you to come down to the station to talk about Donna Barrett. She was a friend of yours, wasn't she?" I keep my tone calm and soothing.

"Donna. I like Donna."

"Great. So could you come here and talk to us about her?"

"Doc Romney is there?"

"Yes, she is."

"I can take the trolley."

"That's great, Bentley. I'm looking forward to meeting you. Donna has said such nice things about you."

"Is Donna there?" he asks. "I haven't seen her. I thought she was sick."

He doesn't know. Or is he repressing the memory of killing her because it's too painful? Since I've never met him, I can't make an educated guess either way.

"No, she's not here, but Doc Romney is."

"She missed our appointment today."

Because she's been in police custody. "She's very sorry about that."

"I'll come. I'll take the trolley," he repeats.

"Good. Thank you, Bentley." I hand the phone back to Drew.

"What do you think is wrong with him?" he asks me.

Judging from the childlike quality of his voice, I'm thinking he has a severe learning disability. "I don't know for sure, but I don't think he's a threat to anyone. He doesn't seem to know Donna is dead."

"Then we have the right killer here at the station. It has to be Cara Romney."

It doesn't have to be her at all. Drew just wants it to be. "We don't know anything for sure. Don't jump to conclusions."

"Don't tell me how to do my job."

We sit in silence for a few moments, at a stalemate.

My phone rings, and I pull it out to see Nolan's picture on the screen. "Hey," I answer.

"Where have you been? I've been trying to call you."

The lower floor must not have reception because my phone didn't even ring. "I'm at the police station with Drew."

Drew shakes his head. "He is not going to be part of this interrogation. No. I forbid it."

"He says hi," I tell Nolan.

"No, he doesn't. Nice try, Syd. Why are you there?"

"He's going to question one of Cara Romney's patients. I think it's best if I'm there since we don't know what this particular patient suffers from."

"Want me to come down there?"

"No, it's fine. I won't be long. I have patients of my own to get back to."

"He told you I wasn't allowed to be there, didn't he?"

The door to the station opens and a small man who really is as cute as a button walks inside. "Nolan, I have to go. The patient just walked in."

"Call me when you're finished," he says.

"Will do." I end the call and stand up.

Drew follows me over to Bentley.

"Bentley?" I ask.

He nods and continues to look around the station. "Where's Doc Romney?"

"She's downstairs right now. Why don't we go find a comfortable place to sit?" I turn to Drew and widen my eyes at him.

"Right this way," he says, leading us to an empty interrogation room.

Bentley is hesitant to enter the small room. "It's tiny."

"Would you like a glass of water, Bentley?" I ask. "Detective Lange would be happy to get you some."

He nods. "With ice."

"Coming right up," Drew says, though his tone conveys he knows I'm getting rid of him on purpose and not merely trying to put Bentley at ease.

I sit down at the table. "These chairs aren't the most comfortable, but they're not so bad," I say.

Bentley sits down. "Doc Romney has a comfy lounge chair. I like that one."

"Does Donna like that chair, too?" I ask.

Bentley shrugs. "She doesn't talk about her visits with Doc Romney."

"What do you two talk about?"

"People. People watching her. She thinks they want to hurt her. I told her I'll protect her."

"You like Donna a lot, don't you?"

"I love Donna. She's my friend."

Loyal, adorable, and a good friend. Donna managed to find one good person in her life. And while she lied about Bentley being her dog, everything else she said about him was true.

I don't want to be the one to tell him Donna is dead. I feel like he'll want Cara present when he finds out. He trusts her. He doesn't know me well enough to be comfortable around me when receiving tragic news.

"Bentley did you talk to Donna Friday night? Did she tell you what she was doing?"

"I talked to her at Doc Romney's on Friday. She said she didn't like spiders. Doc Romney had one of those fake spiders for Halloween. I knew Donna wouldn't like it, so I warned her."

"Don't you have a pet spider?" I ask. "Doc Romney mentioned that to me."

He nods. "Dominic." He says the name slowly like it's difficult for him to pronounce. "Doc Romney said it would be good for me to learn to take care of something, so I got Dominic."

"Did Donna know about Dominic?"

"I told her about him on Friday."

So that's why the spider costume came up in our session. She must have had it on her mind after talking to Bentley.

"I told her Dominic is a nice spider. He doesn't bite me. He crawls on my hand, and it tickles." He laughs.

"He sounds like a very good pet."

"I told Donna she could come over and meet Dominic."

I have to wonder where Bentley lives. He seems to function okay on his own, but where is his family? "Bentley, do you live with anyone?"

"Dominic," he says.

"Do you and Dominic live with anyone else?"

"My mom. She's at work. I'm not supposed to go anywhere but Doc Romney's office without her, but Mom always says to trust police officers. They're the good guys."

That's what made him come here alone.

Drew returns with the water. "Here you go, Bentley." He sets the glass in front of him.

"Thank you," Bentley says.

"Where is he?" a woman shrieks. "Where is my son? You can't question him without me."

"Mom," Bentley says.

Drew gets up and opens the door. "Ma'am, in here."

The woman looks irate. "You can't question him like this. Can't you tell there's something wrong with him?"

"Mrs. Schlater, I'm Dr. Sydney Warner. I'm a friend of Dr. Romney's. I can assure you that I've been with your son since he got here. We were only asking about his friendship with Donna Barrett."

She covers her mouth. "You told him? You told him she's dead?"

As soon as Bentley hears those words, he completely loses it. He starts bawling and pounding his fists on the table. Then he picks up a chair and throws it across the room.

Chapter Fourteen

Drew rushes at Bentley, pinning him against the wall.

"No!" Mrs. Schlater screams. "He doesn't know what he's doing. Please let me calm him down."

"Drew, listen to her," I say, grabbing his arm and staring him directly in the eye. "Please. I'm begging you."

"What's wrong with him?" Drew asks.

"He had an injury to his head when he was eighteen. It affected the normal functioning of his brain and his ability to handle his emotions. That's why he's been seeing Dr. Romney."

"Bentley," I say, "would you like to see Dr. Romney?" I ask.

He stops thrashing at the sound of her name.

"If you agree to sit down nicely, Detective Lange will go get Dr. Romney for you."

"Bentley, you'd like that, right?" his mother asks, moving toward him.

"Yes, Momma."

She reaches for his hand, and I tug at Drew's arm, trying to get him to let go of Bentley. "Come sit with me, baby, and we'll wait for her together."

"Okay, Momma."

I nod to Mrs. Schlater, and she mouths, "Thank you."

I right the chair Bentley threw before leaving the room with Drew.

"Sydney—"

"Detective, that poor man has been through enough. He's going to cooperate, but you have to understand what he's going through is not his fault."

"He needs medical help, not a psychiatrist."

I cross my arms. "Right now, I don't care what you think of my profession or Cara Romney's. That man wants his psychiatrist, and that's what we are going to give him. You know very well that you can't question him without a doctor present."

"Like I said, a medical doctor."

"Drew Lange, I've had it with you. I will act on that man's behalf and file a formal complaint against you if you don't bring Cara Romney up here this instant."

"Is there a problem?" someone says from behind me.

Drew looks over my head. "No, sir, Chief. No problem at all."

Instead of turning to the chief of police, I study Drew's face. He's scared of the chief. "Detective Lange was just about to go get Dr. Romney to help the poor man in the interrogation room. He needs her counseling if Detective Lange is going to get him to cooperate on this case."

"Are you saying Dr. Romney is no longer a murder suspect?" the chief asks.

"I'm not entirely sure, Chief, but I'm legally obligated to allow this man to have his doctor of choice present since he's not of sound mind."

I smile, pleasantly surprised that Drew is giving in.

"Very well. Carry on."

"Thank you, sir." Drew turns and walks downstairs. He doesn't expect me to follow, but I do.

"Can I talk to her for a moment, please. Doctor to doctor?"

He stops at the door and exhales hard.

"Please, Drew." I can tell it's bothering him that I keep calling him by his first name, but I'm trying to establish a different kind of relationship with him. One that isn't based on him being an authority figure. I don't think he sees himself as being human any time other than when he's with Annabelle. It's not healthy.

"You have two minutes, and I'll be right here."

"Thank you." I open the door and step inside the room.

"Is Bentley here? Is that the commotion I heard upstairs?" She looks like she's going to be sick.

"Yes. His mother showed up and thought we told him Donna was dead. When he heard the news, he sort of lost it."

"Of course, he did. That poor man. I don't even know if he took his medication today. He usually takes it in my office when he comes for his session."

I have to say I'm impressed with her level of commitment to her clients. "Look, Cara, I'm going to level with you. I don't think you'd harm one of your clients. You care too much about them. So why don't you tell me what really happened Friday night?"

"I wasn't wearing a flapper dress at the haunted house, but I was wearing a white dress. I was at a formal dinner party when Donna called me."

She left a party to go help Donna. I'm not surprised. "Then I doubt you're the woman that was seen with Donna. Cara, why didn't you just say so? You could have cleared your name from the start."

"Hardly. You saw Detective Lange. He's intent on pinning this on me. Claiming I was wearing a different white dress wasn't going to prove my innocence to him. If anything, the color of the dress might make him more convinced I was the one that person saw with Donna."

"You could invite him to search your place for the flapper costume. He won't find it."

"He'd probably insist I got rid of it. Nothing I say or do will prove my innocence. That's why I asked for a lawyer. It was my best option."

That dress is out there, and so is the woman who was wearing it. "Bentley wants to see you. It was how I got him to calm down. We're going to bring you to him."

"You plan to use me to get information out of him."

"I don't think he harmed Donna."

"I'm not so sure," she says and looks down at her hands in her lap. "I really care about Bentley, so I don't want to believe he'd hurt someone. But he can't control himself when he gets angry."

I've seen that firsthand now. "You think he might have killed her by accident."

She nods. "I can't be the one to make him confess to that. I just can't. I'm sorry. I'd rather go to jail myself than do that to him. He's suffered enough."

"Okay, then don't get him to confess. But he needs to see you right now. He's comfortable with you. Do this for him."

"What if Detective Lange directs me to ask Bentley certain questions?"

"You're not obligated to. You know what's best for Bentley's mental state. Use your degree to get him out of anything you don't think he can handle."

She inhales a shaky breath. "Will you be there, too?"

"If you want me to be."

She nods.

The door opens. "Time's up," Drew says.

"We're ready," I tell him before giving Cara a sympathetic smile.

We head back upstairs, and the second we walk into the interrogation room, Bentley jumps up and throws his arms around Cara.

"Doc Romney!" he exclaims.

"It's so good to see you Bentley," she says. "I missed you this morning. Did you take your pill?"

He lets go of her and shakes his head like he was a naughty child.

"I think I have one in my purse," Mrs. Schlater says, already searching for it. "Here." She pulls it out and hands it to Bentley, who takes it without anything to wash it down. He opens his mouth to show Cara.

"Good work, Bentley. You should feel better soon. I know this is a difficult time for you and me."

"And me," I say. "Donna was one of my patients as well."

"She was my friend," Bentley says, and his hands form fists.

"She was," Cara says. "Would Donna want you to be angry, Bentley?"

He unclenches his fists. "She liked my smile. She said I was cute."

"She did," I say. "She told me."

Bentley blushes.

"That's how Donna would want you to look. Just like that," I say, smiling back at him.

"Why don't we sit down?" Cara suggests. "We can all talk about what we liked about Donna. Wouldn't that be nice?"

It still surprises me that Cara was unaware of Bentley and Donna's friendship. I can see Donna keeping it a secret, but Bentley seems so open with Cara. I can't believe he wouldn't tell her in one of his sessions.

"Bentley, would you like me to start?" Cara asks once we're seated at the table. Mrs. Schlater is beside Bentley, and Drew remains standing, keeping his distance, which is probably a good thing considering he tried to restrain Bentley earlier.

Bentley bobs his head.

Cara places both palms flat on the table. "I liked how Donna always had such good stories to tell."

Stories? Does she know most of what Donna said was lies?

"Did she ever tell you stories, Bentley?" Cara asks.

"She told me secrets. I can't tell you what they were."

Is that why Bentley never told Cara about Donna? Did Donna tell him to keep their friendship a secret? His mother clearly knew about it. "Bentley, you and Donna were good secret keepers, weren't you?" I ask.

He smiles, and he really couldn't look more adorable. He's such a sweet man. "I didn't tell anyone." He leans forward and cups his mouth. "Not even Mamma knows this."

Cara and I exchange a glance. He's not going to betray Donna's trust, even if she is dead. And that means we need to figure out what that secret was on our own and hope he'll assume we already knew it and confirm it for us.

What could it be? I try to remember Donna talking about any men. All that comes to mind is Pierce. But they broke up. Wait.

That's it! They broke up, but she never told me. Is that because she was dating Bentley? Were they romantically involved?

I reach toward Bentley. "Donna didn't tell your secret either, but I figured it out."

Cara eyes me, curious about what I know.

"But we were so careful."

"You were, and I didn't figure it out right away. It took me a while, but you see, I came to know Donna very well."

"Mamma can't know. I'm not allowed to have a girlfriend," he whispers as if his mother can't hear him in her seat beside him.

Mrs. Schlater puts her hand to her mouth.

Cara shakes her head at Mrs. Schlater, indicating she shouldn't say anything. We need Bentley to keep talking.

"I won't tell anyone," I say to Bentley. "Your secret is safe with me."

"I went to Donna's house."

That gives me an idea. "Did you know her neighbor?"

"Eve," Bentley says. "She's not nice. She painted on Donna's fence."

"What did she paint?" I ask.

"A bad word."

Cara holds up a finger. "Bentley, I know you don't say bad words. Could you write it down for us?"

Mrs. Schlater pulls a piece of paper and a pen from her purse and slides it across the table to him.

He looks scared.

"It's okay, Bentley," his mother says.

He picks up the pen. Every moment seems to take an eternity, but he writes the word "liar."

So it's not a bad word itself, but rather Bentley didn't like what it said about Donna. "I see," I say. "What did Eve think Donna lied about?"

"That boy. The one from the supermarket."

"Neil Thatcher?" I ask.

Cara looks at me, clearly never having heard about this before. I quickly catch her up to speed on who Neil is and how he's connected to Donna.

"Why did Eve think Donna lied about Neil?" Cara asks.

Bentley shrugs. "Donna doesn't lie. She's a nice lady."

"Did you see Eve paint Donna's fence?" I ask.

He shakes his head. "Donna told me."

Hmm, it could be another of Donna's stories. I'll need to check with Drew to see if it's true or not. I'd think Donna would alert the police to graffiti on her property.

"Bentley," Drew finally says.

"Don't come near me," Bentley says, getting visibly agitated.

I hold up a hand to stop Drew. "Bentley, I promise Detective Lange won't touch you. He's not going to hurt you."

"He did hurt me. He pushed me." Bentley rubs his shoulder where Drew was gripping him earlier.

"He didn't mean to hurt you," I say. "He was afraid you'd hurt someone when you threw the chair before. But now that he's gotten to know you, he sees you weren't trying to harm anyone. It was a misunderstanding."

Bentley's gaze is laser locked on Drew.

"Detective, what do you want to ask Bentley?" Cara says. "Maybe you could ask me instead so Bentley can see you don't mean him any harm."

Drew lets out a long breath before saying, "When was the last time you saw Donna Barrett?"

"I saw her for her session at my office and then later at the haunted house," Cara says. "How about you, Dr. Warner?"

"I saw her at my office for our session." I look at Bentley. "Bentley, when did you last see her?"

"At her house. She was getting ready to go to a haunted house." He was with her before she left.

"Do you know where she got the costume she wore?" I ask him.

"It was at her house. In her closet."

Why would a woman who was afraid of costumes have the very one we discussed already in her closet? Was it all a lie? Did she lead me in my questioning to suggest the very costume she already had in her possession? I don't know what to make of this woman at all.

Chapter Fifteen

"I don't get it," Nolan says over dinner, which is chicken parmesan over linguini. "Why would Donna date Bentley but insist it had to be a secret?"

"I'm actually not surprised at all by that," I say, twirling linguini onto my fork. "Donna had a warped perspective of the world around her. She saw the worst in people, but Bentley… There's no bad in him. He's such a pure soul. So sweet and caring. I think she recognized that and craved his attention. He was probably the only person in her life who didn't judge her. Who didn't make her feel uncomfortable in some way."

"Okay, I guess I can see that, but why keep it secret?"

"Probably because Cara Romney wouldn't approve of two of her patients dating. I doubt Mrs. Schlater would have liked the idea of her son dating either."

"Wouldn't she want him to be happy?" He forks a bite of chicken parmesan into his mouth.

"I think if she met Donna, she would have seen what Bentley didn't."

I might not have realized that Donna was as disturbed as she was, but I knew she had plenty of issues. Even if she did fool Mrs.

Schlater into believing she wasn't schizophrenic, Mrs. Schlater would know Donna had issues, and considering her son was already dealing with enough, I don't think she would have welcomed Donna as his girlfriend.

"What's your opinion of what Bentley told you about the neighbor?"

"According to Drew, Donna did file a complaint against Eve Driscoll for defacing her fence."

"Why do you not sound convinced that's what happened?"

"I don't know. Something isn't sitting right with me."

"You don't think Donna made up the story about the graffiti on her fence, do you? Or that she actually painted it herself and blamed Eve Driscoll?"

"I wish I knew. I think I need to talk to Eve myself tomorrow."

"Want me to come with you?"

"If you have time, I'd love that. I still need to look her up. I don't know where she works."

"Why don't we go see her after work, then?" he suggests. "We do know where she lives."

That's true, but then what do I do until then? I have my own patients to see, but I'm going to be distracted wondering about Eve the entire time.

I put my fork down and pick up my wine. "You know what would be really nice?"

"Being able to enjoy a meal together without discussing someone's murder?" He smirks.

"Yes, definitely that, but I was thinking it would be really helpful if Donna kept a diary and actually wrote the truth in it."

"Don't you think she'd have to confide in someone?" he asks.

"The problem is I think Donna believed the lies she told. They became her reality, and I don't think she could distinguish between what really happened and what she perceived to be the truth."

"Then a diary wouldn't help," he says.

"No, I guess it wouldn't."

"This reminds me of books and movies that have unreliable narrators," he says. "Like *The Girl on the Train* or 'The Tell-Tale Heart.'"

"'The Tell-Tale Heart' is the closer comparison since the main character tries to claim he's not mad."

"Like Donna didn't think she was mad."

"Exactly. I need to do some digging and find out more about Donna's life before she started seeing me."

"Do you think she experienced some sort of trauma like Bentley did?"

"No, I don't think it's the same thing, but who was she before she moved to Swan Creek?"

Nolan stands up and grabs his plate. "Let's clear the dishes and get to work."

We have dinner cleaned up in about fifteen minutes. Then we go to the living room to start our research. Nolan has a tendency to bring his laptop everywhere he goes. He says he never knows when he'll run into a story, so he likes to always be prepared. We're both seated on the couch with our feet propped up on the coffee table.

Nolan is using his resources from the paper to dig deep into Donna's past while I search her social media profiles. I'm sure most of what she posted was lies, but the photos are a different story. She can't manipulate other people in them, only herself.

I quickly discover a trend with her photographs. They're too perfect. I get an idea and start running a few through image searches. "Bingo," I say.

"What did you find?" Nolan leans toward me to see my screen better.

"Several of her photos aren't really her photos."

"What do you mean?"

"She took them off of Pinterest. She was trying to make it look like she had such a perfect life. Friends, family, nice place to live, pretty belongings. But it's all fake. I found a ton of photos from this one particular Pinterest site."

"Who does it belong to?" Nolan asks.

"Ariel West," I say.

"I'll try looking her up."

I search the Pinterest page and find one photo of a house. "I can't believe this."

"What?"

"Look." I point to the picture. "That's the house next door to Donna's."

"You think Ariel West is Donna's neighbor? But I thought Eve Driscoll was. That's what Drew told you, isn't it?"

"She is. On the other side. They're both Donna's neighbors, and Donna was passing off Ariel's photos as her own."

"That's risky. What made her think Ariel wouldn't find out?"

"She must have saved the images to her computer instead of just sharing them. Ariel wouldn't be notified of that. And they weren't friends so they didn't follow each other on social media either."

"Then Ariel probably has no idea Donna did any of this."

"Probably not."

"Then she wouldn't be a suspect."

I tilt my head from one side to the other. "I don't know. If Donna complained about Eve Driscoll so much, I'm willing to bet she did the same with Ariel."

"There's another possibility," Nolan says.

"What's that?"

"Donna could have been stalking Ariel. Maybe Ariel had the life Donna wanted, so Donna pretended it was hers."

An idea hits me. "We need to look into Ariel West."

"What am I looking for specifically? I can tell you have something on your mind."

"See if Ariel loved old movies, especially those featuring Greta Garbo."

"Are you thinking what Donna told you about that was really Ariel's childhood, not her own?"

"It would make sense. If she knew Ariel liked Greta Garbo, and Donna wanted to be like Ariel, it could explain why she had that dress in her closet. She made sure I brought up the topic in our session and gave her permission to dress the way Donna believed Ariel would on Halloween."

"Wow, the woman was really manipulative."

It's worse than that. "I think on some level, she knew it was wrong to stalk Ariel, so she was seeking my approval."

"But you didn't give her approval to stalk someone."

"No, but I did give her approval to be someone else for a night. In her mind, it was the same thing."

"We need to talk to Ariel West. Maybe even sooner than Eve Driscoll," Nolan says.

"Agreed. I say we get up early and go to her house before she leaves for work."

"Speaking of work, do we know what Ariel does?"

I shake my head. "Let's find out."

We continue to dig into Ariel online. I find her name as an employee at an office on Ninth Street. "Oh, my goodness."

"What?" Nolan asks.

"She works in medical billing and coding."

"Why does that have you looking so freaked out?" he asks.

"Because that's what Donna told me she did."

"Now you're thinking that was a lie, too."

I nod. Who was Donna Barrett really?

Nolan leaves a little before midnight. Everything we learned about Ariel matches what Donna told me about herself. She has a small dog. She was engaged two months ago, but the engagement was recently broken off. That must be why Donna was pushing Pierce to pop the question. She was trying to mirror Ariel's life. When it didn't work, she moved on to Bentley, who she probably thought she could easily manipulate into buying her a ring, only that didn't need to happen because Ariel's engagement was called off.

I don't sleep much because I toss and turn, wondering if Ariel knew Donna was watching her every move.

I'm exhausted in the morning. I sip my extra-large dark roast coffee, which I left black in hopes of it waking me up more, as I drive to Ariel West's house. I'm assuming she works remotely most days, since that's what Donna told me she did. Of course, she also said her boss was pushing for her to go into the office a few days a week, so it's possible Ariel might have to go into work today.

Nolan calls me on the way. He's running about two minutes behind me judging by where he is in comparison to me. I pull into Ariel's driveway, and my gaze goes to Donna's house. There's a white fence surrounding her yard. I wonder where the graffiti occurred. Is it on the side that butts up against Eve Driscoll's yard? That would make it pretty obvious that Eve was the one who did it. But maybe she wasn't trying to hide the fact that it was her.

I wait in my car, drinking my coffee, until Nolan pulls up behind me. I'm assuming Ariel hasn't noticed my car yet because she hasn't come to the door to investigate or so much as looked out a window.

I get out of the car to meet Nolan.

"You look like you slept as well as I did," he says.

"The black coffee didn't even help."

"Mine either." He extends his elbow to me, and I loop my arm through his before we walk to the front door. Nolan rings the doorbell.

A tiny dog barks inside the house, and about thirty seconds later, the door opens. Ariel West is stunningly beautiful. She looks like a movie star. I can see why Donna wanted to emulate her.

"Can I help you?" she asks us.

"Hi, I'm Dr. Sydney Warner. I treated your neighbor, Donna Barrett."

She shakes her head. "Sorry, I don't really know my neighbors. Which one is she?" Her gaze goes from the house on her right to Donna's.

I point to Donna's house.

"Oh. I've seen her a few times. I never talked to her, though."

If they never talked, how did Donna learn so much about Ariel?

"I'm Nolan Lange. I work for the *Swan Creek Gazette*. Your neighbor was murdered last Friday night. We're trying to find out what happened to her."

"That's awful. Did it happen in her home?" Ariel places her hand to her chest and leans out the door to get a better look at Donna's house.

"No, it wasn't on her property," Nolan says.

"You didn't know her at all?" I ask.

Ariel shakes her head. "Sorry, but no."

"Ms. West, could we come inside for a moment?" I ask her. "I think we need to talk."

"I'm not sure what about."

"Your neighbor was suffering from schizophrenia, and we believe she was pretending to be you."

"Me? But she didn't even know me."

I take out my phone and pull up Donna's social media profiles. "She posted these photos of her house," I say, turning the phone toward Ariel.

Ariel's mouth drops. "Those are my photos."

"We know. That's why we're here."

She steps back. "Come in."

We walk inside, and I recognize the interior of her home from the pictures online.

"Why did—I mean how did she do this? She's never been inside my house."

"We're not sure. Has anything ever gone missing?"

She brings us to the living room. "Do you think she broke in here?"

"Maybe. Or she could have taken the photos from your Pinterest page," I say.

Ariel paces the space in front of the fireplace. Then she suddenly stops and snaps her fingers. "There was a mishap with the dry cleaner. I had this dress I was planning to wear for Halloween. I was going as Greta Garbo, but when I went to pick it up, the woman at the desk told me the dress had already been claimed. I told them that couldn't be because I had my ticket. They didn't know what happened. They couldn't explain it, but they had an identical ticket from when the dress was claimed."

That's why Donna was at the laundromat where Kevin Richman worked. She was picking up Ariel's dress.

Chapter Sixteen

This case is getting more disturbing by the minute. I meet Nolan's gaze, and he looks just as weirded out as I feel.

"What's going on?" Ariel asks us. "Do I need to call the police? Is this a case of identity theft or something?"

"As much as I hate to say it, calling Drew might not be a bad idea," I tell Nolan.

He nods and takes out his phone.

"Who is Drew?" Ariel asks me as Nolan makes the call.

"Detective Lange with the Swan Creek Police Department is Nolan's brother. He should be able to help us figure this out."

Ariel squeezes her hands together. "I guess I shouldn't be so scared. I mean the woman is dead, so it's not like she's going to hurt me, but did she really take my dress?"

"She was wearing it when she was murdered."

Ariel's hand flies to her mouth. I reach out to steady her because I'm afraid she's going to faint or something. This must be a huge shock to her system.

"Why don't you sit down?" I say. "Can I get you a drink or something?"

She walks over to the chair by the fireplace and sits. "No. I don't want anything. I'm just so confused and overwhelmed."

I crouch down beside her chair. "That's completely understand-able."

"Why me?" she asks.

"I don't know. She must have seen something in you that she admired."

"I know the expression says imitation is the highest form of flattery, but this is too much. It's not flattering at all. It's scary."

"Drew is on his way," Nolan says, pocketing his phone. "He's nearby, so it should only be a few minutes until he arrives."

Ariel looks at me. "You said this woman was a patient of yours."

"Yes, but she lied to me. I had no idea she was schizophrenic. She was actually seeing a psychiatrist for that. I'm a psychologist. I don't prescribe medication. I help my patients talk through their problems."

"I'm aware of what you do. I see a psychologist myself."

That doesn't shock me. It's probably why Donna started seeing me. "How long have you lived here?" I ask, but I think I already know the answer.

"About a year and a half."

The same amount of time that I've been seeing Donna. Exactly as I thought.

"Is that important?" she asks.

"I don't want you to worry about it. This is a lot for you to take in."

She takes a few deep breaths and then asks, "Is it wrong that I don't feel bad that she's dead? I mean, I did when you first told me, but now… All I can think is that this woman was watching me. She must have been if she somehow duplicated my dry cleaning ticket."

"Ariel, you're entitled to your feelings, whatever they are. It's okay. You don't have to apologize for them or feel bad about them."

She bobs her head in understanding. "Thank you. I appreciate you listening."

"Ariel, if you don't mind my asking, what do you see a psychologist for?"

"Post-traumatic stress disorder. I was abused as a child."

"I'm so sorry."

The doorbell rings.

"That must be Drew," Nolan says. "Ariel, you stay. I'll get it." He turns and walks from the room.

When Nolan returns, he's whispering to Drew. Drew approaches Ariel. "Ms. West, I'm Detective Lange with the SCPD. Would you mind telling me what you believe happened with your neighbor, Donna Barrett?"

Ariel takes a few deep breaths. I wish I could tell Drew for her, but I know he needs to hear it straight from the source. Once she's finished, her hand shakes. I place mine on top of it to steady her. I'm still crouched beside her, trying to offer as much support as I can.

"Detective, Donna seemed to know an awful lot about Ariel. I think you might want to sweep her house for any signs that Donna was in here." I don't want to come out and say that Donna might have planted a recording device in here because I know Ariel will freak out at that suggestion, but that's what I'm thinking.

"Dr. Warner, would you accompany me?" Drew asks.

Nolan narrows his eyes at me, but I'm just as surprised as he is that Drew wants my help.

"I'll be right back," I assure Ariel before standing up and following Drew out of the room.

"Lay it all out for me," he says.

"Donna was trying to be Ariel. It was Ariel's dress Donna was murdered in."

"How did Donna get it? Do you think she broke in here?"

"No. Or at least not for the purpose of stealing the dress. She picked that up herself from the dry cleaner."

He steps into the kitchen and turns to me. "The laundromat where she got that kid from the youth center fired."

"Yes."

Drew furrows his brow. "That doesn't add up. If she was trying to get away with impersonating Ariel, why would she make a scene? I'd think she'd wave the incident off as an accident and get out of there before anyone figured out she wasn't Ariel West."

"I thought the same thing at first. But you have to remember that Donna was suffering from schizophrenia. We don't know what would set her off. It's possible the accident confused her, and she acted out in the moment, forgetting she was supposed to be Ariel."

"Do you think she knew she was pretending to be Ariel?" Drew asks. "Or did she really believe that's who she was?"

"It's quite possible she merged her sense of self with Ariel. I don't think she could separate the two in her mind."

"But she didn't have people call her Ariel," he says.

"She didn't need to. She fully believed they were the same person."

Drew rubs his forehead. "This is all new territory for me."

"Let me put it this way. If she believed she and Ariel were the same individual, then she wouldn't see anything wrong with coming into this home or using Ariel's photos online or picking up Ariel's dry cleaning."

"All right. I think I'm following. I know the bank didn't find any kind of security system in Donna's house, so she wasn't watching her that way."

"I have an idea." I walk back to the living room. "Ariel?" I ask, and I wait for her to look up at me before I continue. "Do you lock your doors at night?"

"Yes, always."

I knew it was a long shot. Victims of abuse tend to be overly guarded. They wouldn't be able to fall asleep without having all the doors and windows locked. But Donna was getting in here somehow. Unless…

"Nolan, when you researched Donna, did you find any indication that she was good with computers?"

He shakes his head. "She dropped out of school at sixteen."

"Donna Barrett was abused as a child," Drew says. "I've been looking into her past."

Donna was abused just like Ariel. Did Donna somehow figure out Ariel was a victim of abuse and that's what caused her to want to be like her? That commonality between them? I'm willing to bet Donna dropped out of school at sixteen because that's when the effects of the abuse she suffered caused the onset of her schizophrenia.

"Ariel, were your online passwords ever changed without your doing?"

"Yes, about a month after I moved here, I got several notifications that my passwords had changed. My credit card number had been stolen prior to that so I assumed it was some sort of security breach with an online company I placed an order through."

If Donna got into Ariel's email and then changed her passwords, she probably had access to everything Ariel did online, at least for a little while.

Drew jots that down in his notebook.

"Here's what I believe happened," I say. "Donna found out about your past, Ariel. That's what drew her to you. You were both abused as children. But you must have seemed like you had your life together compared to her, so she tried to emulate you. Over time, she came to think of you two as the same person."

Ariel's face goes completely pale. "I think I know how she did it."

I move toward her again, wanting to offer support. "Take your time."

"When I first moved in, my realtor left me a basket on my front porch. It contained some baked goods, a congratulatory card, and the keys. She told me she left me two sets of keys, but I only ever found one. I thought they must have fallen out somewhere."

"But now you think Donna took the second set," I say.

"I remember her car was in her driveway when I first got here. I'm pretty sure she was home."

And Donna is the type to snoop. If she went to see what was on her neighbor's front porch, she might have taken the keys.

"Why would she steal someone's keys?" Drew asks.

"She was very paranoid. Maybe she planned to check out her new neighbor," I say. "And later, when she'd merged their two lives in her mind, she had keys to let herself into Ariel's house whenever she wanted."

"She probably read my diary."

I'm guessing she read the diary the first time she was inside the house. It was probably how she discovered Ariel was abused.

Drew moves toward Ariel. "Ms. West, I appreciate your cooperation. We're going to give you some time to yourself, but if you think of anything else that might be helpful, please give me a call." He hands her a business card.

"I know you already have a therapist, but my door is always open if you need a listening ear," I tell her.

"Thank you."

"We'll see ourselves out," Nolan says.

Drew stops outside his patrol car and clears his throat. "Thanks for calling me." He bobs his head once and then gets in his car and drives away.

Nolan looks like he's in shock. "You heard that, right?"

"I did." I have to get to my office before I'm late for my first appointment. "See you at lunchtime?" I ask him.

He nods, still in shock that his brother actually said thank you.

I'm more than a little surprised when Drew Lange calls me at lunchtime. "Drew, to what do I owe this call?"

"I wanted to give you a heads-up."

That's new. "About what?"

"The only one who makes sense as the murderer now is Bentley Schlater."

"Bentley?" I yell. "No. He makes the least sense. He loved Donna."

"You saw how he flung that chair. Dr. Romney said if he doesn't take his medication, he can't control his emotions."

"I know, but it's not him. Please, Drew. You have to trust me on this. Figuring out Donna was trying to be Ariel is important."

"How? I don't think Ariel killed Donna. She'd have to be a very skilled actress to pull off a performance like that."

I agree that Ariel's reaction and emotions were genuine. "I'm not arguing with you there. But it explains the dress Donna was wearing and why she was at the laundromat. Things are finally starting to fall into place."

"Except we still don't know who killed her."

"Nolan and I are going to Eve Driscoll's house at six today. Why don't you come with us?"

"Why are you still working this case?"

"Do you really want to waste time asking stupid questions like that? Donna was my patient. She was in much worse shape than I thought."

"But if she lied to you, why do you care who killed her?"

"She was a person. A sick person who needed help."

"And you failed to help her," he says, but his tone isn't accusatory. He says it like he actually understands how I feel.

"I owe it to her to figure this out."

"Six o'clock," he says before hanging up.

Lena knocks on my door before opening it. I swipe at a tear that escapes my left eye. "Hey, Lena," I say. "What's up?"

"I wanted to remind you that I have to check out early today for a dentist appointment."

"Right. No problem." I'd completely forgotten she was leaving early. I've had too many other things on my mind. "Lena, before you go to lunch, can I ask you a question?"

"Of course. Shoot."

"What did Donna Barrett usually do in the waiting room before her sessions?"

"She was on her phone like everyone else."

Figures. She was probably using the time to check Ariel's social media profiles so she'd have something to talk about in our sessions.

"Great. Thanks."

"This is really bugging you, huh?" she asks.

"Kind of, yeah. I'm sure the police will sort it all out in no time, though."

"I can't believe it's been almost a week. Tomorrow is Halloween."

"I know. Crazy, right?"

She wags a finger at me. "I thought that word was taboo in here," she teases since I don't let my patients use that word to refer to themselves. Needing to talk to someone does not make anyone crazy. It's completely normal to want to be heard. I'd be more inclined to use the word crazy to describe someone who doesn't want to talk about their problems. Though, truth be told, I still wouldn't because usually those people want to talk but don't feel they can for a variety of reasons. So yeah, I don't allow the use of the word in my office.

"I take it back," I say. "Enjoy your lunch."

I grab my things and head to the diner where I'm meeting Nolan and Autumn. Aaron is holding down the fort at the youth center, which is allowed to reopen this weekend since the CSI team will officially be finished with the crime scene whether the case is solved by then or not. Aaron is showing Kevin the ropes and getting him ready for his new role as a counsellor to the younger kids.

When I enter the diner, I spot Nolan and Autumn already seated at a corner booth. I point them out to the hostess, who hands me a menu and tells me I can go join them.

"Hey," I say, slipping into the booth beside Nolan, who kisses my cheek.

Autumn sips her coffee. "You didn't tell me your boyfriend was so funny," she says.

"He has a lot of great qualities. That's just one among many." I smile at Nolan, who blushes. Being adorable is high up on that list of good qualities.

"Before I left, Drew called me," I say as I flip over the coffee mug in front of me. The waitresses here have coffee vision. The second a cup flips, a waitress magically appears at the table with a pot of coffee.

"What did he want?" Autumn asks, her tone reflecting her opinion of Drew.

Nolan looks down at his menu.

"He wanted to move Bentley Schlater to the top of his suspect list, but I told him how absurd that is. Then I invited him to talk to Eve Driscoll with Nolan and me later today."

Nolan puts down his menu. "I'm glad I wasn't drinking coffee when you said that, or Autumn would be wearing it about now."

Autumn laughs. "See? He's funny. Of course, it wouldn't have been funny if he actually did spit coffee on me." She brushes off the front of her white dress shirt. "This top cost a small fortune."

"I thought you were saving money for your future," I say. Autumn has been on a baby plan since February. First, she wanted a house to raise a baby in, which she now has. But Aaron wants to make sure they have enough money in savings before they start trying to get pregnant.

Autumn bobs one shoulder. "I had some birthday money from my parents, so I decided to splurge."

"What made you invite Drew along?" Nolan asks, but before I can answer, the waitress returns to take our orders.

I wait until she's gone before getting to his question. "I figured it's best to keep an eye on him so he doesn't go making the situation worse."

"He let Cara Romney go," Nolan says.

I turn in the seat to face him. "You talked to him. Why didn't you tell me?"

"It's nothing. I called him at the station to see if he wanted to pool resources to look into Donna's background. He told me he released Cara. It wasn't a long conversation. He turned down my offer."

I place my hand on his leg. Nolan keeps reaching out, and Drew shuts him down every time. I'm sure after Drew thanked us at Ariel West's house, Nolan thought they'd begun to chip away at that wedge that's been between them for the past thirty-one years.

There's a commotion at the bar top, and all three of us look in that direction. One of the waitresses uses the remote to turn up the volume on the TV mounted to the wall.

"Local resident, Bentley Schlater was arrested moments ago for attacking a sixteen-year-old boy inside ShopSmart."

"Neil!" Autumn yells, jumping up from her seat.

Nolan and I don't hesitate to run out after her.

158

Chapter Seventeen

Speeding isn't smart to begin with, but speeding in the direction of the police station is really stupid. Nolan is pulled over by Officer Cardell, who we sort of have a history with considering he was supposed to watch us while we were in police custody several months back, and we slipped out without him knowing.

Officer Cardell taps his knuckles on Nolan's window, and Nolan lowers it. "License and registration."

"Officer Cardell," I say, "you know us. We're trying to get to Detective Lange. It's about the case he's working on."

"License and registration," he repeats.

Nolan rolls his eyes and pulls the documents from his wallet. "Here. When you call it in, be sure to tell my brother that you're the one holding me up."

It's an empty threat since Drew has no idea Nolan is on his way to the station. Drew didn't call and ask Nolan to come down. And the fact that another reporter beat Nolan to this story has to sting right now on top of everything else.

Officer Cardell takes the documents back to his car.

Nolan pulls out his phone and dials Drew. "Officer Cardell pulled me over. Syd and I are on our way to you right now. Can you please call him off?"

I lean toward Nolan so I can hear Drew's response. "I'm busy," is all he says before ending the call.

"Why did you answer then?" Nolan screams into the phone. He drops it into his lap. "He's always going to be like this, isn't he?"

"Only Drew can answer that for sure. But he did thank you. That's something. And he answered your call. He might have done that because he was afraid you were in trouble. But you can't expect him to change overnight."

"How about over eight months? That's how long I've been back in his life. Eight months and all it amounts to is a thank you."

"Did you ever think you'd get that much from him?"

He scoffs. "No. But it's so little I can't even feel the least bit encouraged by it."

Officer Cardell returns with Nolan's ticket. Nolan takes it and gets back on the road without a word. Autumn is already at the station when we pull in. It scares me that she didn't wait in her car. Autumn isn't the type to think through what she wants to say before she spewing it out at the person she's angry with. In this case, that person is Drew Lange, who has handcuffs on him at all times.

We hurry inside the station. Autumn is being detained at the front desk.

"You are not the boy's mother. I'm not letting you back there. Now you can leave quietly, or I can show you to a lovely holding cell where you can cool off." The woman at the front desk crosses her arms.

I take Autumn by her shoulders and pull her back. "Autumn, let's go see Detective Lange."

"Detective Lange is busy at the moment," the front desk officer says.

"Can we wait for him at his desk?" I ask.

"Be my guest, but if she tries anything funny, I will throw her skinny behind in a holding cell." She wags a finger at Autumn.

I tug Autumn toward Drew's desk. "Have you called Neil's foster mother?" I ask her.

"I can't get through. I doubt Detective Lange did either, which means Neil is in there by himself. That's not even legal! He's a minor!" She yells the last two comments so everyone can hear.

The front desk officer marches toward us, unclipping her handcuffs at the same time.

"Nolan, hold her," I motion to Autumn, and I step toward the female officer. "I'm Mr. Thatcher's psychologist. I was present the previous time he was questioned. I'm requesting to be present now as well. Detective Lange will allow it."

She stops and reclips her handcuffs. "Follow me, but you're not getting inside that interrogation room unless Detective Lange tells me it's okay."

"Very well," I say. "Though being that he's a minor, Mr. Thatcher and his foster mother can press charges if Mr. Thatcher doesn't have an adult present on his behalf."

She huffs at me and starts toward the interrogation room. She knocks on the door. "Detective Lange, I have a psychologist here who says she's the boy's doctor."

"Doc Sydney!" Neil shrieks.

"See," I say to the female officer.

She opens the door.

"How did I know you'd show up?" Drew says, but he motions for me to have a seat.

I smile sweetly at the female officer before she closes the door behind me. I sit down across from Neil. "Are you okay?" Before he can answer, I turn to Drew. "Where is Bentley?" I'm not sure who I'm more worried about right now.

"Dr. Romney is with him. We had to call her in after we handcuffed him. We were afraid he'd be a danger to himself. She brought some medication to help him calm down."

Poor Bentley. I know what happened. He got it in his head that Donna's death was Neil's fault because he believed what Donna told him about Neil.

"Neil, I want to apologize. Bentley was involved with Donna Barrett. She told him about you and the restraining order. I think he believes you killed her."

"I didn't do anything to that woman."

"I know." I reach across the table and take his hand. "We'll get this sorted out." I turn to Drew. "He's not in trouble for anything, right? He's the victim."

"We're just trying to piece together what happened since Bentley is in no condition to talk to us," Drew says.

I bob my head. "Neil, can you tell us what happened?"

"I was at work, stocking shelves in the chip aisle. That guy stormed up to me. He had my picture in his hand. It was my employee photo from the store. It was on the wall because I was employee of the month back in August." He looks down at his lap. "That's why my boss didn't really fire me when he told Donna Barrett he would. I'm a good worker."

"So, Mr. Schlater tore your picture off the wall?" Drew asks.

Neil bobs his head. "One of my coworkers, Barry Ipsen, said Bentley came in asking where to find me. Barry pointed to my picture to show him what I looked like, and Bentley ripped it off the wall and came looking for me."

Drew scribbles this down in his notepad even though I'm sure this is being recorded. Or can he not record since Neil's foster mother isn't present? I'm not sure how that works.

"He held up the picture and asked me if that was me. Then he grabbed my arm and yanked me away from the shelf. I hit the shelf behind me, but he caught me before I fell and then tossed me into my cart of chips I was stocking. That's when Barry jumped in and tried to break up the fight."

Bentley isn't a big man by any means, and even though Neil is a sixteen-year-old kid, I'm not sure Bentley has the strength to pull this off. "Neil, you refused to fight back, didn't you?"

He nods. "I could tell by the way he talked that something wasn't right with him. I didn't want to hurt him. I think he was just confused."

"You're a good person, Neil," I say.

"Can I go now?" he asks Drew.

"We're still trying to get in contact with your foster mother."

"Good luck with that." Neil rolls his eyes. "I bet she got your message and just doesn't care. She only took me in for the money. She files for all these reimbursements, saying I ate all this food and cost her all this money, but it's bogus."

I turn to Drew. "If that's true, you need to look into it."

He scowls at me. "Do I tell you how to do your job?"

"She's not going to come down here. She'll pretend she didn't have service and didn't get your call. Do I really have to wait? I need to get back to work."

"Autumn is here. I'm sure she'll drive you," I say.

Drew sighs. "Okay, go on," he tells Neil.

Neil jumps up and rushes out of the room.

"Thank you," I say.

"He was the victim. He's been through enough."

"Can I see Bentley?" I ask, getting to my feet.

"I told you Dr. Romney is with him. I don't think you going to see him is going to help anything."

Bentley probably does need time. "Will you at least tell Dr. Romney that I'm offering my services if she thinks it will help Bentley?"

He nods and motions for me to exit the room.

Autumn and Neil are gone by the time we return to Drew's desk.

"Thanks for your help back there with Officer Cardell, Bro," Nolan says, his voice full of sarcasm. "I appreciate you having my back."

"You broke the law, Nolan. That's on you."

"Right because I'm just another resident of Swan Creek to you." He turns and walks out of the station.

I meet Drew's gaze. "Here's some free advice. You lost thirty-one years with him already. Thirty-one years that you could have had his support, his love, and his adoration. He's not the only one you're punishing by keeping him out of your life." I turn on my heel and walk out to Nolan's car. I get in and click my seat belt without saying a word.

Nolan is focused on the road. "Still hungry?" he asks.

"I bet our food's ready by now," I joke.

He doesn't laugh.

"My first afternoon patient will be at the office soon. You can drop me off at the diner so I can get my car."

Nolan drives to the diner in silence and kisses me goodbye. "Sorry I'm not better company."

"Still my favorite company, whether you're quiet or not."

He gives me a weak smile before I get out of the car.

I drive back to the office, my mind on Bentley. I hope Cara can help him.

I'm not sure if Drew will show up at Eve Driscoll's house after what happened this afternoon. He and I were starting to at least form a truce, but after what I said to him, he might not want to see me, even if it will help the case.

Nolan picks me up at home so we can take one car to Eve's house. There's no car in the driveway when we arrive, so I get out of the car and walk over to Donna's fence.

Nolan follows me. "What are you looking for?"

"Evidence of the graffiti." I run my hand over the paint. "Does any part of the fence look like it was repainted recently to you?"

We inspect the entire length on the side of Eve's house, but it all looks the same. Nolan walks around to the front of the fence.

"Hey, check this out," he calls to me.

I meet him at the front gate. "The gate is slightly brighter." I run my fingertips over it. "It feels smoother, too."

"Donna probably had to sand the darker paint in order to get the white to cover it completely," Nolan says.

"So Eve, or someone, definitely defaced it."

"It seems that way," he says. "Hopefully, she comes home soon."

We get back into his car to wait. About five minutes later, a patrol car pulls up alongside us. The window lowers, and Drew says, "I take it she isn't home yet."

"No, not yet," I say, unsure if Nolan will respond.

"How long have you been waiting?" Drew asks.

"About twenty minutes," I say.

"I didn't think you'd show," Nolan finally says.

"I had some paperwork to finish up with before I could come. Looks like I didn't miss anything." He gestures in front of us. "I'm going to pull up head of you."

I guess that's the end of the conversation. Still, maybe what I said to Drew at the station had some small impact on him. Of course, there's always the possibility he's afraid Nolan and I will solve this before him and that was his real motivation for coming along.

We wait another half hour before a car approaches. It slows when it sees the patrol car, but it pulls into the driveway. A woman gets out, and so do Nolan, Drew, and I.

"Can I help you?" the woman asks.

"Are you Eve Driscoll?" Drew asks, holding up his badge even though I'm pretty sure she figured out he's a member of law enforcement from the police car he arrived in.

"I am. Who might you be?"

"I'm Detective Lange. I'd like to ask you a few questions about Donna Barrett."

"Sure. I'd be happy to tell you about that nut job."

"Hey!" I yell. "Ms. Barrett had an illness. Don't call her names."

"I don't know about an illness, but she tried to press charges on me for something I didn't do. You can look at her track record. It speaks for itself. The woman had a few screws loose." Eve Driscoll looks to be about Nolan and my age, maybe a few years older, but she talks like she's got about twenty years on us. It's strange.

"How long have you lived next door to Ms. Barrett?" Drew asks.

"I don't know. A few years now I suppose."

"And you two didn't have a good relationship?"

Eve scoffs. "The woman called the cops on me multiple times for noise violations. No one else in the neighborhood ever complained. Only her."

"What about the graffiti on Donna's fence?" I ask.

"You mean the word she painted on the fence and blamed me for?" Eve scoffs. "I think she was mad because she hadn't been able to call the police on me in so long, so she made up a problem to report me for."

"You're saying she lied?" Drew asks.

"Yeah, that's what I'm saying. The woman is a liar for sure."

"Funny because that's the word someone painted on her fence," Drew says.

"If you ask me, she knew she was lying. That's why she chose that word." Eve crosses her arms.

"You mentioned her track record," I say. "What do you know about that?"

"I've heard people talking about her. How she yells at everyone. I heard she made a scene at the laundromat, too. Got some poor kid fired."

"Were you there when it happened?" Drew asks.

"I've got a laundry room in my house. What do I need a laundromat for?"

"Dry cleaning," I say. "Two of your neighbors went there for that purpose. Why not you?"

"I work in construction. I don't exactly have any attire that needs dry cleaning," Eve says.

"That must be tough," I say. "I bet you work with a lot of older men."

"You win that bet." She uncrosses her arms. "I had to learn not to take grief from anyone."

"I'm sure you did. You seem like you can hold your own." She's not a big woman, but I'd guess she's stronger than she looks.

"I do okay. I'm a good worker, so I earned the respect of everyone else out there with me."

"When was the last time you saw Donna Barrett?" Drew asks.

"I see her practically every day. We're neighbors after all." She leans onto the trunk of her car. "Look, I'm not going to lie and say I'm sorry she's gone. The woman caused me a lot of grief. But I don't know anyone who actually liked her, so I can't say I'm surprised she got herself killed."

That's a common reaction on this case. Most of the people in Donna's life can understand why she wound up dead. Everyone except for Bentley.

"Did you know Bentley Schlater?" I ask.

"Is that the man that used to come to Donna's house?"

I nod. "He's a small man."

"Oh, that one."

"Who were you referring to?" Drew asks.

"Some guy. I don't think I've seen him in a while, but he was tall and built."

She must be referring to Pierce Crawford, Donna's ex.

"But you've seen both men before?" I ask.

"Yeah, it made me wonder how a woman like Donna got one man let alone two."

Was she seeing them simultaneously? I was under the impression Bentley came after Pierce.

"Were they here around the same time?"

Eve lets out a deep breath. "Let me see. I don't think they were ever here on the same day. The smaller guy was a little later, not by much, though. He seemed off to me. Like he wasn't all right in the head."

"Did you ever talk to him?" I ask.

"Nah. I avoided Donna completely. That included her men."

"Did you happen to go to the haunted house at the youth center last Friday night?" I ask.

"Not really my thing. I think stuff like that is for kids, you know?"

This is getting us nowhere.

"That guy was here last Friday, though. I saw him. He didn't seem happy when he left Donna's place. I thought maybe they'd had a fight or something."

Drew's gaze flits to me, and I know exactly what he's thinking. Bentley killed Donna, and afterward he felt so guilty that he went after Neil to try to make it up to her in spirit.

Chapter Eighteen

I'm suddenly regretting having invited Drew along. Eve Driscoll is making Bentley Schlater look even guiltier in Drew's eyes. I don't think Bentley did this, though.

"Thank you for your time, Ms. Driscoll," Drew says, heading back to his patrol car.

"Happy to help," she says.

Nolan and I follow Drew.

"That's it," Drew says. "I'm going to have no choice but to hold Bentley until I get a warrant to search his place."

"Drew, listen to me. If it is Bentley, and let me be very clear when I say I don't believe for a second that it is, he would have had to plan the murder ahead of time. You've seen him. His brain injury doesn't make him capable of such a thing. He acts in the moment. When he went after Neil at the grocery store, he didn't bring a weapon of any kind. A man that small wouldn't go looking for a fight without arming himself in some way."

"But he clearly did go looking for a fight," Drew says. "That's why he was at the food store to begin with."

"Something must have provoked him right then and there."

"How are we supposed to find out what that is?" Drew asks. "You have no idea how difficult it is to get any information out of him."

"Let us help you," I say. "We'll go with you to interrogate Bentley. You'll need to make sure Dr. Romney is present of course. And Bentley's mother."

"This sounds more like a social gathering than an interrogation," Drew complains.

"That doesn't sound like a no to me," I say.

"Nine o'clock. Sorry if you both have work, but I need to close this case."

"We'll be there," Nolan says.

Drew nods and gets into his patrol car. We watch him drive away.

"Can you cancel your morning sessions?" he asks me.

"I won't need to. The office is always closed on holidays. Even Halloween."

I arrive at the police station at a quarter to nine. Not that I think Drew would try to start early to get information out of Bentley before Nolan and I arrive. First, I don't think he'll get anything out of Bentley. I think only Cara Romney and I can do that.

Drew is at his desk, and he waves me over. "My brother isn't with you?" he asks, not looking up from his paperwork.

"We drove separately."

"And here I thought you two did everything together these days. I was going to ask when the wedding was."

"If things were that serious, you'd know. You see, unlike you, Nolan wouldn't get married without at least inviting his brother to the ceremony."

Drew closes the file in front of him and meets my gaze. "Don't act like he wishes he had been at my wedding."

"He does. How can you not see that? It was a slap in the face that you didn't even tell him you were getting married. It's not like he expected to stand up there with you and be your best man—though I'm pretty sure that's what brothers are for. He just wanted you to acknowledge him."

"Are you saying you two might get married one day?" he asks.

"I'm not saying anything other than you hurt him."

He clears his throat. "For what it's worth, I think you two should get married. You're good for each other." He stands up and walks over to the water cooler.

Nolan comes into the station and makes a B-line for me. "Where's my brother?"

I point, unable to speak.

"Are you okay? What did he say to you?" Nolan looks ready to punch Drew in the face for upsetting me.

"I'm surprised. He said he thinks we're good together."

Nolan looks at Drew, who only acknowledges him with the barest movement of his head. "He said that?"

I nod. "Strange, right?"

"Very."

Drew comes back over to us. "You ready? We're going to Bentley's holding room."

"Room?" I ask.

"Dr. Romney said a cell would only agitate him further. He's in the room downstairs."

We follow Drew down the stairs and to the same room where Cara was held previously. She's already inside with Bentley. When we enter, she turns to greet us as if this is just a social call and not an interrogation, which I'm sure is how she wants Bentley to see it.

"Good morning, Bentley," I say. "It's good to see you again."

He gives me a small wave.

"Bentley, you remember my friend, Dr. Warner," Cara says.

He nods. "She's pretty," he whispers to Cara.

"She is," Cara replies.

"Thank you, Bentley. I think you're very handsome," I say.

He blushes.

"Bentley, we'd like to talk to you about Neil Thatcher," Drew says.

Bentley's face gets beet red. "He hurt Donna."

"Bentley, breathe," Cara says. "Remember what we talked about."

"Bentley." I move closer to him. "We think there was a misunderstanding between Donna and Neil. He didn't really try to hurt her. Donna was confused. I know Neil." I place a hand on my chest. "He's a good kid. He assured me he never hurt Donna, and I know he wouldn't lie to me."

"She said." Bentley clasps his hands together and squeezes tightly. "She said."

"Who said what, Bentley?" Cara asks.

He raises one finger to his lips. "It's a secret. I can't tell the secret. Not supposed to tell."

I get an idea. "Okay, you don't have to tell us the secret. Just tell us who told you the secret."

Bentley looks at me, and I can tell he's trying to decide if that's okay. "Donna. She told me to go after the boy at the food store."

"When did she tell you to do that, Bentley?" Cara asks.

"Yesterday."

Cara, Drew, Nolan, and I all look back and forth at each other. What Bentley is saying can't be true. Donna's dead. She couldn't have talked to Bentley. He must be confused. It's possible he's having trouble letting go so he's pretending to talk to her. He's probably running through old conversations they had, replaying them in his mind.

"Detective, I'd like to speak to you in private," Cara says. She looks at me. "You should come."

I nod and stand up.

"Bentley, Nolan is going to stay with you while I talk to Dr. Warner and Detective Lange, okay?" Cara asks him.

"Do you have pretzels?" Bentley asks.

"There are some in the vending machine," Drew says.

"We'll bring you back some pretzels, Bentley," Cara says with a smile.

He grins as we walk out.

"Detective, I think this has all been too much on my patient. If he thinks Donna is talking to him…"

"You're going to recommend his lawyer pleads insanity, aren't you?" Drew asks her.

"If you pursue him as the killer, then yes. I'll have no choice but to declare him as not being of sound mind. He's a very sick man."

Drew walks over to the vending machine at the end of the hallway, and we follow. I'm pretty sure he's gathering his thoughts. He puts money into the machine and presses a few buttons. Then he bends down to retrieve the pretzels, which he hands to Cara. "I understand your patient is sick and that he's your main concern, but my responsibility is to Donna Barrett. I have to bring her killer to justice. Now that may look different for Bentley, given his situation, but I still owe it to the victim to solve the crime. That's my duty."

"I understand," Cara says. "But he also hasn't confessed to killing Donna."

"Would he?" Drew asks.

"Maybe. I'm not sure."

It's possible Bentley would be so overcome with grief and guilt that he might tell us what he did, but it's also possible he's repressed the entire thing.

"I'm going to get a warrant to search his place," Drew says.

Cara nods. "Let's not explain to him what's happening yet. I see no reason to upset him like that unless you find something incriminating."

Drew considers it for a moment before nodding. "I think this interrogation is over for now. I need to go get that warrant in motion."

Cara nods to each of us and returns to the room where Bentley and his mother are waiting. Nolan and I follow Drew upstairs.

"Go home. There's nothing for you two to do here." Drew rubs his brow before sitting down.

"Can I call to have food delivered for you or something?" Nolan asks him.

Drew looks up in disbelief. "Um, no, that's okay. The warrant will take some time. I'll get the ball rolling and then go home to eat."

Nolan shoves his hands in his pockets. "Okay. Goodnight then."

I loop my arm through Nolan's as we walk out of the station. "I think that went pretty well."

"I'm not convinced Bentley did this," Nolan says.

"Oh, I'm not either. I was talking about you and Drew. That was the most civil I've seen you two be toward each other."

"I suppose."

We get in the car, and he drives me home. He doesn't cut the engine when we get into my driveway, though.

I unclick my seat belt and turn toward him. "What's going on?"

"Do you mind if I don't come in? I'm kind of beat."

"Okay, yeah. No problem." I lean across the middle console to kiss him goodnight. "Call me tomorrow."

"Thanks, Syd."

I get out and walk to the door. Nolan waits for me to get inside the house before he leaves. I give a small wave, which he returns. I take a hot shower before even thinking about dinner. It feels like such a long day. My heart breaks for Bentley. I don't want him to be the killer. What happened to him is awful. I take some comfort in the fact that Drew seems sympathetic to Bentley's situation. He didn't push him in the interrogation, and he even bought him pretzels. Somewhere deep inside, the man does have a heart. But I also think it was Drew's empathy for Bentley that upset Nolan so much. Seeing his brother able to care about a stranger but not him must hurt. I wish I could fix their relationship, but unless Drew wants to fix it, there's not much Nolan or I can do.

After my shower, I heat up some leftovers in the fridge and sit down in the living room with my notebook from my sessions with Donna. Now that I know everything was a lie, whether Donna was aware of the lies or not, I'm not sure what I'm hoping to find.

The woman thought she and Ariel were the same person. So how does Bentley factor in? He seems to be the piece that doesn't fit into this puzzle. I put the notebook aside and look up Ariel West online. If Donna wanted to be Ariel, then there has to be a clue in Ariel's social media profiles.

I keep searching. Ariel has tons of photos, which makes sense since she's young and very pretty. It takes me about two hours, but I find a photo of Ariel with a man who appears to be a few years older than her. They're both wearing sunglasses and sun hats. The caption on the photo says, "I love you, Joseph."

"Who is Joseph?" I ask the air. Ariel didn't tag him in the photo, which means he might not have his own social media profile. I look for other pictures with him in them, but that's the only one I find.

I throw "Ariel West Joseph" into my search bar in hopes Google will do its thing and find a connection for me. I have to scroll through a few pages before I find Ariel's birth announcement in a newspaper. It mentions her older brother, Joseph West.

Next, I search Joseph West specifically, but that proves to be problematic since it's a common name. The number of results the search yields would take me days to go through.

My doorbell rings, making me jump. Did Nolan feel bad for leaving and decided to come back? "Just a second," I call out, putting my laptop on the coffee table and standing up.

I answer the door to see Autumn holding a white box and a bottle of wine.

"I brought reinforcements."

I step aside to let her in and close the door behind her. "Reinforcements for what?"

"Nolan called me. Well, he called Aaron. He said he had to leave you to handle the case on your own and that you might need my help. Oh, and I'll be staying the night. I hope the sheets in the guest bedroom are clean."

I take the white box from her. "They are. Thanks for coming. And what is this?"

"Just some marble cheesecake since you missed out on it last time."

"You are the best."

"I really am." She sets the wine on the center island and grabs the bottle opener from the drawer. She pours two glasses while I get us each a slice of cheesecake and put the box in the fridge, which is looking very empty at the moment. When was the last time I went grocery shopping? I should really go in the morning.

We take our cake and wine into the living room, and I fill Autumn in on what I've been doing.

"Joseph West is definitely not a unique name," Autumn says. "I can see why you're having trouble finding him. Maybe keep trying to find him with Ariel's name in the search as well. At least her name isn't all that common."

"Good thinking." I take another big bite of cheesecake before pulling my laptop onto the couch with me and trying the search. It's still not going well. "I found their parents' names: John and Monique."

"What's with this family?" Autumn asks around the cheesecake in her mouth. "The men have the most common names, yet the women get pretty and rather unique names."

"I don't know, but I have an idea." I use Joseph's name and his parents' names in my search this time. "I found his birth announcement." I scan it, and I shouldn't be surprised by what I found. "I probably should have expected this."

"Expected what?" Autumn leans closer to read my screen. "Joseph was born mentally handicapped?"

I nod and get idea. I do another search, this time for facilities where severely mentally handicapped individuals can live with around-the-clock care. "Bingo. He lives in a home for people who can't take care of themselves due to mental and physical handicaps."

"What does this mean, Syd?"

"It means Donna somehow found out about Ariel's brother, and she formed a relationship with Bentley as a way to be more like Ariel."

"Does that help the case at all?" she asks.

"Well, Bentley doesn't seem to be as bad off as Joseph, but the fact that Donna cast him into this particular role means she could have slipped up and called him Joseph. She thought she was Ariel. While she never called herself that name, she might have made mistakes when it came to other people in her life."

"You think calling Bentley Joseph could have upset him to the point where he'd kill her?"

"I'm not saying I believe that's what happened, but I think Detective Lange might."

Chapter Nineteen

Autumn is still asleep when I wake up Friday morning. I really need some food in the house, so I get ready and head to ShopSmart. The store is pretty empty at this hour on a Friday. It might be a holiday, but it's not one that closes schools or most businesses. I decided to close for all national holidays when I first opened my practice, but I know it's not typical. Still, some of my patients are kids, and I know they don't want to go to therapy on Halloween. It's a day when they should be carefree and trick-or-treating. By being closed, it assures their parents can't cut into their fun by bringing them to my office.

I grab a cart and start loading up on produce. I make a mental note to always food shop in the early morning like this because I feel like I'm getting first dibs on all the good stuff. The store is being fully stocked with fresh fruit and vegetables. I buy way more than usual, but I can always pack salads for my lunches during the week, so I'm not worried it will go to waste.

When I reach the cold foods aisle to get bacon and eggs for breakfast this morning, I see Neil Thatcher. "Good morning, Neil."

"Hey, Doc. What are you doing up so early?"

"Well, it seems I've let my refrigerator go empty."

He bobs his head. "So you're shopping before work?"

"No, I'm actually off today."

"That must be nice. I work seven days a week most of the time."

"Are you saving for college?" I ask, opening a carton of eggs to make sure none are cracked.

"Here, take these." Neil hands me an extra-large carton. "They're on sale this week, and I just checked them for cracks."

I close the carton I was inspecting and take the one he's offering. "Thank you. I can't help noticing you avoided my question."

He looks down at the stack of eggs on his cart. "College isn't an option for me. My foster mom already said I need to find a job and get my own place as soon as I graduate high school. That's just over a year and a half away, so I figure I better save up as much money as I can. Apartments aren't cheap."

"Maybe you and Kevin Richman could get a place together and split the cost of rent and utilities," I suggest.

"He's staying at the youth center now. I doubt he'd want to leave that. It's rent-free."

"I think that's just a temporary solution until he gets back on his feet. You should talk to him about it."

"Excuse me," a woman says behind me.

I turn to see it's Eve Driscoll, one of Donna Barrett's neighbors. "Eve, nice to see you again."

She gives me a curt smile. "Good morning, Neil. Got any good eggs on that cart for me today?"

"Oh, sure." He grabs an extra-large carton and hands it to her. "Here you go, Ms. Driscoll."

"Please, call me Eve."

Neil nods, but I know he's going to continue to call her Ms. Driscoll. He's too polite not to. He calls Aaron and Autumn by their first names, but that's because Autumn and Aaron insist on the kids at the youth center using their first names.

"I hope you don't mind me saying, but I couldn't help overhearing you mention not going to college."

How long was she standing near us if she heard that? The last thing we talked about was getting an apartment.

"There are plenty of scholarships you could apply for. In fact, my company gives out a scholarship to one student every year. Here, let me give you my card. You can give me a call, and I'll get you the information. You're a junior, right?"

"Um, yeah."

"Great. This is the perfect time to apply then." She unzips her purse, pulls out her wallet, and removes a card, which she hands to Neil. "Don't wait too long. If you call me this weekend, I can get you the necessary paperwork to fill out. I'll even walk you through how to do it all."

"Um, thank you. You really don't have to do that," Neil says, taking the card from her.

"It's my pleasure. I've seen you here for a while now. I can tell you're a hard worker."

"Thank you," he says, putting the card in his shirt pocket.

Eve smiles at him before pushing her cart down the aisle.

"That was really nice of her," Neil says.

"It was. Did her card say where she worked?"

He pulls it from his pocket. "Um, it just says Driscoll Technologies."

So she has her own business. If it's her business, I wonder if she's the one who awards the scholarships each year. Neil might be a shoe-in considering how much Eve seems to like him. "You should apply."

"I don't know. I think she was just being nice. I mean, she's the one who helped me out when Donna Barrett accused me of stalking her. Ms. Driscoll went to my boss and said she saw the whole thing and I didn't do anything to Ms. Barrett."

"Why not try anyway? It can't hurt, right?"

"I guess not." He stares at the card. "I suppose the worst that can happen is I keep working here and have to get a tiny studio apartment. That's where I'm heading if I don't apply, so you're right. There's no downside to trying."

"Good." I smile and pat his shoulder before continuing down the aisle.

After checking out and driving home, I unload the groceries and start on breakfast. I make the bacon and omelets with green pepper, onion, and American cheese.

"Mmm, what smells so heavenly?" Autumn asks, walking into the kitchen looking very sleepy. She pours herself a cup of coffee before sitting down at the center island.

"That would be our breakfast."

She sips her coffee. "I'm telling Aaron I may not come home if he doesn't start pampering me the way you do."

I laugh. "Great. He'll be mad at me for sure."

"He's probably staring at the carton of eggs right now, wondering how to make them magically transform into an omelet."

"Come on. He's not that bad. I've seen him cook before."

"He has about three dishes he knows how to make, and one of them is pasta, which is basically just boiling water."

"What are the other two?"

"Rice from those little pouches, which again is boil water and stir, and heating up already prepared frozen meals."

"I really thought he could cook more than that," I say, flipping the omelet in the pan.

"Nope. It's all me."

I remove the bacon from the oven and plate it. By then the omelets are finished, so I plate them up as well. I sit down beside Autumn, and we dig in.

"Yeah, I'm not leaving unless Aaron buys me something pretty." She points her fork at the omelet on her plate. "This is too good to give up for any less."

I laugh and continue eating. The doorbell rings a few minutes later.

"Who is that?" Autumn asks. "I don't even have any makeup on."

I look through the peephole to see Nolan standing on my front porch. "Nolan."

"Oh, he doesn't matter."

"Um, that's my boyfriend you're talking about."

"Exactly. *Your* boyfriend. I don't care if my morning, pre-make-up face scares him."

I open the door. "Hi, stranger."

He steps into the house and kisses me hello. "Mmm, it smells fantastic in here."

"You can't have any," Autumn says. "Syd only made two omelets."

"I'll share mine," I tell him. "Have a seat."

"Good morning to you, too, Autumn," Nolan says, sitting down in my seat.

I grab another plate, cut the omelet in half, and place it on the plate. "Orange juice or coffee?" I ask.

"Coffee. Black please."

I pour his coffee before sitting down. "So, I found out Ariel West has a mentally handicapped brother."

"That explains Bentley's presence in Donna's life," Nolan says. "Drew will have a field day with that. I called the station on the way here. Drew got the warrant to search Bentley's house. Mrs. Schlater insisted on being there during the search."

"Did you ask if we could tag along?"

"I did. I'll let you guess how that went."

"Of course, he said no," Autumn says.

But the slight smile on Nolan's face tells me otherwise. "He said yes!" I blurt out.

"Shocking, right? I nearly crashed my car into a tree when he told me."

"When?" I turn to look at the clock on the stove. It's almost nine.

"Ten o'clock."

"Great, so we can finish breakfast first."

"Darn," Autumn says. "I was hoping you'd have to go so I can eat yours, too."

I cock my head at her. "Is there something you're not telling me?" She brought wine over last night, so I don't think there's a possibility she's eating for two.

"No, I'm just really enjoying having someone else cook for me for a change."

We finish breakfast, say goodbye to Autumn, and head out to meet Drew at Bentley's house.

"What did you say to him?" Nolan asks me on the way. "And before you try to deny it, I know you must have said something at the station when you stayed behind."

I take a deep breath. "I told him he wasn't only punishing you by keeping up this wall between you two. I guess he realized I was right."

"Well, he's not exactly acting like the picture-perfect big brother, but he's being much more cordial. It's a start."

"You guys have a lot to get past. It makes sense that it will take some time."

His grip on the steering wheel tightens. "Thanks for helping."

"Any time." I place my hand on his leg.

Drew's patrol car is in Bentley's driveway when we arrive. He's already inside, though. Apparently, we're allowed to tag along, but we don't merit waiting for. Baby steps.

We get out of the car and head inside. The front door is wide open. Mrs. Schlater is in tears in the hallway, a tissue clutched in her hand. I walk over to her.

"Can I do anything for you?" I ask.

"Get them to stop accusing my son," she says. "He didn't do this. He couldn't have. There's no way he was dating that woman."

"I don't think he was. I think Donna saw him more as a brother."

"I'm not sure if that's much better."

"What I'm saying is I don't think she was trying to take advantage of Bentley in any way. I think she liked to talk to him." And she needed him to play a role in the life she imagined. All that talk about people who dress up in costumes being liars and Donna being put off by it all, maybe it was something deep inside her that rejected what she was doing. The part of her who still knew who she really was. Maybe she was really afraid of herself. She could have been confessing to me in her own roundabout way in hopes that I'd save her from herself. And I failed her.

"Mrs. Schlater, would you please come in here?" Drew calls from Bentley's bedroom. From the tone of his voice, I know he found something incriminating.

Nolan and I follow Mrs. Schlater into the room, which is almost completely bare. The walls are white and so is the furniture, which is very minimal. A bed and a dresser. That's it.

Drew is standing at the bed. "I found this in the pillowcase." He holds up a paper.

We step closer, and I see it's a flyer for the haunted house at the youth center. From behind the flyer, Drew pulls out a picture. A picture of Donna and Bentley staged to look exactly like the one of Ariel and Joseph that I found online.

I suck in a breath.

"What is it, Sydney?" Drew asks, noticing my reaction.

This is not going to help Bentley in any way, but I have to tell Drew what I know. If I don't, Drew will do his own digging around until he finds the photo, and then he'll probably arrest me for withholding information. I take out my phone and locate the photograph of Ariel and Joseph. I turn the screen toward Drew. "This is Ariel West, the woman Donna Barrett wanted to be. And that's her mentally handicapped brother, Joseph."

"Oh, dear," Mrs. Schlater says. "Bentley mentioned someone named Joseph. I didn't know who he was talking about."

Drew turns to Mrs. Schlater. "How would your son react if Donna called him Joseph by mistake?"

Her hand flies to her mouth, and she sobs. "Getting people's names wrong is one of his triggers. So little makes sense to him, but names he knows."

"So he'd get very upset by it," Drew says.

Mrs. Schlater nods. "I need to call a lawyer."

Chapter Twenty

I'm really surprised Mrs. Schlater hasn't called a lawyer until now, but I guess she thought her son's condition and Cara Romney's diagnosis of him would be enough to protect him. After seeing the flyer for the haunted house, that picture of him and Donna looking like Ariel and Joseph, and figuring out Donna slipped and called Bentley by Joseph's name, Mrs. Schlater is convinced her son accidentally killed Donna in a fit of rage.

Drew brings everyone back to the station, including Mrs. Schlater's lawyer and Cara Romney. He calls in Autumn and Aaron as well. I can tell he's determined to close this case once and for all right now.

Autumn sits next to me in the conference room. "What is this about?" she whispers.

"I'm not entirely sure."

The only one not present is Bentley.

"Okay, let's get started," Drew says, standing at the head of the table. "We found evidence in Bentley's room, in his pillowcase to be precise, that implies he attended the haunted house."

"Circumstantial," the lawyer, a man named Rosencranz says.

"I'm aware of that. And I'm aware that this crime also appears to have been premeditated, which is why I've called the Youngs here. Mr. and Mrs. Young, we've identified the murder weapon as a knife from the kitchen in the youth center."

"What?" I ask, looking at Autumn. "Why didn't you tell me that?"

"I thought you knew," she says, her gaze going to Drew. "Did you not tell Sydney that on purpose?"

"Dr. Warner is not a detective working this case. Besides, as her best friend, it seemed likely you'd mention that fact to her at some point."

It's obvious he hoped Autumn would assume I'd know, which is exactly what happened.

"My point is this. Since the murder weapon was at the crime scene and not brought in by the killer, it stands to reason this was in fact a crime of passion, one committed in the heat of the moment."

"Did the haunted house go through the kitchen?" I ask Autumn since Nolan and I never got to finish going through it last Friday night.

She nods. "I didn't think to lock up the knives. Why would I?"

I reach for her hand. "No one is blaming you."

"I am," Mrs. Schlater says. "If you'd taken more precautions, my son wouldn't be a suspect right now."

"That's speculation," Drew says. "He could have bludgeoned her or strangled her instead. There's no way to know."

"No one is saying Bentley harmed anyone," Rosencranz clarifies. "He has not confessed to anything."

"Which is why I want to establish a few things before I speak with Bentley," Drew says.

"What things?" Mrs. Schlater asks.

"We know that Bentley believed Donna Barrett was his girl-friend. He's told us as much. But Donna thought he was her brother. He was playing the role of Joseph West, Ariel West's handicapped brother. Mrs. Schlater, you've already said that Bentley was upset last Friday night because Donna called him Joseph."

"What time was that?" I ask, interrupting him.

Rosencranz holds up his hand. "I'd like a word with my client."

"Your client is Bentley Schlater, not his mother," Drew says, losing patience.

"I-I don't know what time it was. I got home late that night. That's when he told me, but he didn't say when it happened," Mrs. Schlater says.

"Did you know Bentley had plans that evening?" I ask.

"No. He didn't tell me. He knew I would have said no if he'd asked to go out. He usually snuck out to see Donna, mostly when I had to work. He knew how to take the bus or trolley. The drivers all knew him. That was my fault. I insisted on introducing them to him in case of an emergency. You know if something happened while I was at work."

"It seems to me that you've been underestimating your son's capabilities, Mrs. Schlater," Drew says. "No matter. I can call the trolley and bus companies to find out if any drivers remember Bentley going to the youth center that night."

There's nothing the lawyer can say to that. If a driver puts Bentley at the scene of the crime at the approximate time of the murder, things are going to look bad for him.

"I'm going to question your son. I understand you'll want to be present with your lawyer, and seeing as how I'm a reasonable man, I'll allow Dr. Romney and Dr. Warner to also be present."

Drew is covering his own butt. He's trying to show that he acted sympathetically. But his end goal is still the same. He plans to lock up Bentley for this murder. It will be in a psychiatric ward instead of a prison, but it's still an end to the case for Drew.

Mrs. Schlater is sobbing now.

"Mrs. Schlater, Bentley needs you to be strong for him when we go in there," Cara says.

I couldn't agree more. Seeing his mother so upset might trigger one of his episodes, and that's only going to prove that he lashes out when he's upset. "The best way to help your son right now is to remain as calm as possible so he doesn't get agitated. Can you do that?" I ask her.

"I'm going to need a moment to compose myself," she says.

"Of course." I stand up. "Detective Lange, might I suggest we all leave and allow Mrs. Schlater a few moments to herself?"

He dips his head toward the door, dismissing everyone else.

Autumn hugs me before leaving. "Good luck. This is just so awful."

It is. What's really awful is that there's not more we can do for people like Donna and Bentley.

"Hey." Nolan wraps an arm around me. "Don't go beating yourself up over this."

"It's hard not to. I might not have known Bentley, but I should have realized Donna was lying to me. The problem was that she'd convinced herself her version of reality was real, so she didn't display the typical signs of being dishonest."

"Exactly, so you can't blame yourself, Syd."

"He's right," Autumn says. "Please don't do that. You help so many people, Syd. You couldn't help Donna because she wouldn't let you."

I nod to appease them, but looking back now, I realize Donna left me a ton of clues. There was a part of her that hated herself for denying her own identity and replacing it with Ariel's. She actually confessed to me the only way she knew how, by claiming a fear of the things she was doing to herself.

Aaron and Autumn leave after I assure them I'll be okay.

"I didn't get an invite to this interrogation," Nolan says. "I'll be right here at Drew's desk waiting for you."

I nod.

Drew walks over to us. "I'm sorry, Sydney. I really am, but I have to see justice served."

"I know you're only doing your job, and I appreciate how you're handling Bentley."

Drew's gaze rises. "Mrs. Schlater came out of the conference room. She must be ready to get this over with."

I take a deep breath and give Nolan one last look before following Drew downstairs to the room where Bentley is being detained.

He smiles when he sees his mother. "Momma."

"Bentley." She rushes over to him on the small bed and wraps him in a hug.

Cara and I exchange glances before sitting down at the small table in the room.

"Hello, Bentley," Cara begins.

"Hello, Dr. Romney," he says. "You brought your friend."

"Hi, Bentley," I say.

"Bentley, I brought a few friends to speak with you. They'd like to know what you did last Friday night. Do you remember that night?"

Bentley looks down at his lap. "I don't want to talk about it."

Drew stiffens beside me.

"Is that because Donna called you by the wrong name?" Mrs. Schlater asks.

Bentley bobs his head and starts crying. "I'm not Joseph."

"No, of course not," Mrs. Schlater says.

"What happened after Donna called you Joseph?" Drew asks.

Bentley cringes when he hears the name again.

I get up and walk over to him. "Bentley, Donna needs your help. Do you want to help her?"

He nods. "I tried. I tried to hurt the boy who hurt her."

"Neil Thatcher didn't really hurt her, though," I say. "It was a misunderstanding."

"Did you see Neil at the haunted house on Friday?" Drew asks.

Bentley nods, and the lawyer groans. "You tricked him into admitting he was there."

It was an underhanded move by Drew. I turn and glare at him. "You could have asked him if he was there."

"How is it any different?" Drew asks.

"Bentley, why did you go to the haunted house that night?" I ask.

"To protect Donna."

"From whom?"

"She said that boy was watching her again. She said he was supposed to be fired but wasn't. She saw him."

"Did you find Donna in the haunted house?" I ask, and Cara gives me a look. She's not happy I'm helping Drew. I'm trying to help everyone involved, though. We need to know what happened.

Bentley nods again. "She was in the dark room with the machine."

The asylum room. Bentley confirmed he was in the room where Donna was murdered.

"She didn't like that I was there. She yelled at me and shoved me. She called me Joseph." He starts sobbing uncontrollably.

"Detective, that's enough," Cara yells. "I want everyone out of here so I can calm him down."

But Drew's not finished. "Did you go into the kitchen after that and grab a knife? Did you use that knife on Donna?"

"Bentley, don't answer that," Rosencranz yells.

All the yelling is only making Bentley get more upset. He starts thrashing on the bed, and his mother has to stand up to avoid being hit.

Drew gives her a look. "That's all the proof I need that he lashes out when upset, and he was clearly upset that night."

"He didn't hurt me," Mrs. Schlater says. "He doesn't know what he's doing."

I push Drew from the room. "Enough. You can't question him anymore. Can't you see what you're doing to him?"

"What I see is a deeply troubled man. I feel for him. I do. But he murdered a very disturbed woman."

And his loyalty on this case is to Donna. "I get it. I know you want to find Donna's killer."

"No, you don't get it, Sydney. I already have found her killer. I'm arresting Bentley Schlater for the murder of Donna Barrett."

Chapter Twenty-One

"Please come," Autumn says. "It's Halloween, and it's our grand reopening. You have to come to support the kids. Kevin and Neil will be here. So will Mario. They all asked for you."

"Now you're just playing dirty," I say.

"Come on. Put on that female Mad Hatter costume, get that man of yours who thinks Clark Kent is somehow cooler than Superman, and get your butts down here. I'll tell everyone you're on your way." She hangs up before I can protest more.

The doorbell rings almost instantly. I pocket my phone and answer it. "Nolan, what are you doing here?" He's dressed as Clark Kent, so the answer is pretty obvious.

"Autumn called me."

Most likely before she even called me. She knew I wouldn't be able to say no to Nolan if he picked me up already in costume. "I'm not dressed, and I really don't feel like going out tonight." I'm still upset about Bentley. I know all signs are pointing to him being guilty, but I hate it.

"Let's go for a little bit. You want to support Autumn, Aaron, and the kids at the community center, right?"

"That's not why you're trying to convince me. You know if I sit here alone, I'll pour over my notes from my sessions with Donna and reach for straws trying to prove Bentley didn't kill her."

He takes my hand in his. "What can I say? I know you well."

"Fine. I'll go get dressed and make an appearance, but I'm not staying long."

"Whenever you want to leave will be fine with me." Before I can say a word, he adds, "As long as we actually show up first and talk to the people we're going there to support."

My face falls. He does know me well if he anticipated my reaction to leaving whenever I want. I turn and walk toward my bedroom. My costume is hanging in the closet, so I grab it and slip it on. I don't feel up to doing my full makeup, so I do the bare minimum and call it good enough. I put my hat on to complete the outfit and walk back out to the living room, where Nolan is seated on my couch.

"That was quick," he says.

"The quicker we go, the quicker I can come home." I grab my phone and keys from the small table in the foyer.

Nolan opens the door for me, locking it behind us. "I'm sorry things didn't work out the way you wanted them to," he says once we're on the road.

I know part of my problem is that I'm questioning myself. How I missed things that now seem obvious. I know there wasn't much indication that Donna was lying about practically every aspect of her life, but it still hurts.

"I'll be okay. I'm sure Cara Romney will do everything she can to help Bentley."

"You know what the saddest thing about all of this is?" Nolan asks.

I can think of plenty of sad things, but I narrow my eyes, unsure where he's going with this. "What?"

"No one seems to feel bad for Donna. She's the one who died, yet everyone else is appearing more like victims than she is."

He's right. Ariel's identity was practically stolen. Neil Thatcher was falsely accused of being a stalker and almost lost his job. Kevin Richman did lose his job because Donna lied and threatened to press charges against the laundromat if they didn't fire Kevin. Eve Driscoll may or may not have been wrongly accused of graffiti. I'm still not sure on that one. Pierce Crawford basically thinks he dodged a bullet by ending the relationship with Donna. Not a single person is saying poor Donna.

"But then there's you, Syd." Nolan looks at me for a second. "Donna probably lied to you more than anyone, yet you were out there trying to find her killer for her. You didn't have to do that. Look at all the effort you poured into this case. She had no idea how lucky she was to have you for a therapist."

"Thank you. I really needed that."

He takes my hand and brings it to his lips to kiss the back of it.

The haunted house is even more packed than the previous Friday night. I don't know if it's because today is Halloween and people who are too old to trick-or-treat are looking for some scary good fun, or if the fact that someone was actually murdered inside the haunted house is what's drawing the crowd. Either way, the youth center must be making good money from this.

We wait in line, but the second Autumn sees us, she waves us to the front. "Syd, Nolan, get over here. You're not paying to get in."

"Of course, we are. It's for a good cause."

"We probably wouldn't even be open if not for you two, so you've more than paid your share." She dips her head toward the door. "Besides, you paid the first time and didn't even get to walk through the whole haunted house."

"See you on the other side," I tell her with a wave.

"That's the spirit," Nolan says, taking my hand in his.

"Are you being sweet or are you scared of walking through the dark, spooky youth center?" I ask.

"Quite possibly both," he teases.

We make it through the graveyard scene where the body pops up out of the coffin and tries to grab people. Then we go to the room with the scary clowns. I see Kevin in his costume with his rubber knife. He jumps out at me but waves in the process, ruining the effect of being scary.

"A killer who waves hello before attacking his victims," I say. "It's definitely a bold choice, Kevin."

He laughs. "I couldn't help myself. Everything is going great with this job. I've never been happier, and Neil called me earlier to ask if I'd get an apartment with him once he turns eighteen. It will be a while, but it's nice to have a plan for the future."

"That's great, Kevin. Neil's a good kid."

"Yeah, he told me about some scholarship he's applying for. He sounds pretty excited."

I'm glad he's going to go through with trying for the scholarship even though he thought it was a long shot.

"Well, I got to go scare some people," Kevin says with another wave.

Nolan and I walk toward the asylum room. I can see the flashing lights, which means the high voltage machine is on since it's the only light in the room. There are screams and then some laughter.

"That's my favorite part," a woman says, and I recognize the voice.

I turn around and can just make out what appears to be a white flapper-style dress. I grab Nolan's arm. "Look. I think that's the woman who was with Donna right before she was murdered."

Nolan looks all around, but the room is completely dark again. "I didn't see her."

"I thought it sounded like…Eve Driscoll."

"What would she be doing here?" Nolan asks. "Didn't she say she was too old for haunted houses?"

"She did." I leave the asylum room, tugging Nolan with me.

"Where are we going?" he asks.

"To look for Neil."

"Why Neil?"

"I have a bad feeling."

"Syd, what is going on? Is Neil in trouble?"

"I don't know." We enter the kitchen, which is next to the asylum room. It's staged with a dead body on the table, sausage links spilling out like intestines. There is barely any light, just from the candelabra on the table by the body. "Eve is the one who told Neil about the scholarship. She even offered to help him fill out the paperwork. And she stuck up for him when Donna tried to get him fired."

"Then what makes you think she'd hurt Neil? It sounds like she's looking out for him."

She is! "Nolan, why would a woman in her early thirties look out for a sixteen-year-old boy?"

"Maybe because he's a foster kid, and she feels bad for him."

"Yeah, and she would feel very bad if he's in foster care because of her."

"What do you mean?"

A flash of white in the dark corner of the room draws my eye, and I push Nolan aside as Eve Driscoll lunges with a knife. I scream, but I know no one is going to come to my rescue since plenty of people are screaming inside this haunted house.

"I should have known you'd figure it out," Eve says, advancing on me.

Nolan fumbles, looking for a light switch, and I move to the other side of the table, keeping the fake dead body between us.

"You're his biological mother, aren't you?" I ask.

"What gave it away? The nose? It is a distinctive nose."

That is partially what tipped me off. "Mostly it was the way you treated him at the food store. There is no scholarship, is there? You made it up. Your plan was to pay for his college education without telling him who you really are. But why?"

"Why?" she asks. "Seriously?"

A few kids come into the kitchen with us and point to what's going on. They think this is part of the haunted house. That Eve and I are acting out roles. I have to get them out of here so Eve can't hurt them. "Leave!" I scream.

"Why can't I get the lights on?" Nolan asks, trying to get to us. Eve whirls around, thinking Nolan is going to try to wrestle the knife away from her.

Without thinking, I race around the table and shove her from behind. I hear her fall even though I can barely see inside the room.

"Dude, this is intense," a kid says.

"Turn on the lights!" I yell.

"I got it." The lights come on, and Neil is standing in costume, staring at us.

Eve's eyes go to him. "Neil."

"Ms. Driscoll?" he asks.

She gets to her feet. Nolan positions himself between her and Neil, not letting her get any closer to him.

"Get out of my way."

"Not happening. Hand over the knife. It's over, Eve. Sydney and I both know you killed Donna Barrett."

"Yeah, a wretched woman. I'd never hurt my own son." she throws her arm out in Neil's direction.

"You mean me?" Neil asks. Now that the lights are on, I can see how pale he looks, and not from his costume makeup. "You're my mom? Is that what you just said? Is that why you're always around wherever I am?"

"Neil." Eve drops the knife, and Nolan grabs it immediately.

"I had to protect you. That woman was out to destroy you. I couldn't let her do that. I couldn't give you the life you deserved when I had you. I was barely older than you are now. I thought you'd be better off with another family. But she wouldn't leave you alone."

"You killed Donna Barrett?"

Eve moves toward Neil, who backs up. "Baby, please. I had to. There's nothing I won't do to protect you. I've been watching over you your entire life."

"If you've been around and have enough money to offer me a fake scholarship, why didn't you tell me who you are and get me out of the foster system?" he asks, his voice full of anger.

"I'm no mother. I know that. You would have hated me. But this way, you thought I was a nice lady who helped you out. It was better."

"What I think is you're crazy. You killed someone who didn't even get me in trouble. My boss knew she was making it up. There was no need for any of this. Stay away from me. I don't want your money. I don't want anything to do with you."

Eve falls to the floor and sobs at Neil's feet, begging his forgiveness.

Nolan has his phone pressed to his ear. "It's Eve Driscoll. She just tried to kill Sydney inside the haunted house and admitted to killing Donna Barrett. We have her in the kitchen now, and she's no longer armed."

He called Drew. He was in trouble, and he called his big brother.

Nolan lowers the phone. "He's on his way," he tells me.

"What's going on?" Aaron rushes into the room.

"We need to lock this room. No one in or out," I say. "Eve Driscoll killed Donna Barrett."

I've never been so happy for a holiday to be over. Drew arrested Eve and released Bentley. Bentley is going to have to go to a facility to help with his anger management and his grief over the loss of Donna. But I'm confident Cara Romney will see that he gets the care he needs.

Neil Thatcher is going to be my newest patient. After finding out Eve is really his mother, he wants to work through his feelings on the subject. I'm not charging him for the sessions. He's going to help out around my office instead. I want him to continue saving his money so if he wants to go to college, he'll have the option when the time comes.

Autumn and Aaron took the haunted house down immediately after Eve was arrested, and they've vowed to never host one again. Autumn said next year will be all about face painting and fun corn mazes instead.

Drew called Nolan and me down to the station to go over our statements one more time. Nolan opens the door for me, and we head for Drew's desk. He's on his computer, typing away, a pencil between his teeth. He looks up when he sees us and removes the pencil from his mouth, tossing it on top of his desk. "Have a seat."

I can't think of what we need to go over again, but I'm not going to stop a meeting between the brothers.

"Drew, before we get into the case and the paperwork you need us to sign, I want to thank you," Nolan says. "When I called you last night, you didn't ask questions. You believed me when I said Eve was the killer."

Drew leans forward and laces his hands on his desk. "You're not a liar. You're not a lot of the things I've accused you of being in the past." He pauses, and I know this is difficult for him to say. "I'm sorry I've blamed you for all these years."

Nolan swallows so hard I hear it. "It's okay."

"No, it's not. I'm not saying I'm ready for weekly family dinners or anything, but well, I don't know where to start if I'm being honest."

"You already started," I say. "You showed up when Nolan needed you last night."

Nolan nods, and so does Drew.

"I wanted to thank you both. Thats why I called you in. The case is closed. We're finished here."

"Oh." Nolan's face falls, and I realize he thinks Drew means he's finished with him.

"Nolan, I don't think Drew is finished with his train of thought."

Nolan looks at his brother.

"Next time I get a big case, I'll call you to cover it. That is if you'd want to work with me again." Drew clears his throat.

"Yeah, absolutely. I'll be there."

Drew starts typing on the computer again as if the conversation is over.

Nolan and I stand up.

"Good work, Detective," I say.

He looks up and gives us the tiniest of smiles.

Nolan places his hand on the small of my back and walks me out. "Wow," he says once we're back in the car. Is it weird that I think things might actually get better between us?"

"Weirder things have happened. And you are Clark Kent, after all, reporter extraordinaire."

He smiles. "Thanks, Syd. For the first time ever, I'm leaving this station happy with my brother. I can't tell you what that means to me."

"Then let's go celebrate," I say.

"As long as it's not with another haunted house."

"No. Something much better. Let's hit up all the half-price sales on the Halloween candy," I say with a smile. "That's how adults celebrate Halloween."

If you enjoyed the book, please consider leaving a review. And look for *Christmas Corpse*, coming soon!

You can stay up-to-date on all of Kelly's releases by subscribing to her newsletter:

ABOUT KELLY HASHWAY

Kelly Hashway fully admits to being one of the most accident-prone people on the planet, but luckily, she gets to write about female sleuths who are much more coordinated than she is. Maybe it was growing up watching *Murder, She Wrote* that instilled a love of mystery, but she spends her days writing cozy mysteries. Kelly's also a sucker for first love, which is why she writes romance under the pen name Ashelyn Drake. When she's not writing, Kelly works as an editor and also as Mom, which she believes is a job title that deserves to be capitalized.

Acknowledgments

Many thanks to my editor, Patricia Bradley. Your feedback is always so valuable and immensely appreciated. To my family and friends, thank you for continuing to be so supportive of my writing career.

To my VIP reader group and ARC team, thank you for your help spreading the word about my books. And to my readers, thank you for making time for my books and characters.

ALSO BY USA TODAY BESTSELLING AUTHOR KELLY HASHWAY

Holidays Can Be Murder Series:
Valentine Victim
Fourth of July Fatality
Halloween Homicide

Traumatic Temp Agency Series:
Corpse at the Candy Shop
Tragedy at the Toy Shop
Bludgeoning at the Boutique

Piper Ashwell Psychic P.I. Series:
A Sight For Psychic Eyes
A Vision A Day Keeps the Killer Away
Read Between the Crimes
Drastic Crimes Call for Drastic Insights
You Can't Judge a Crime by its Aura
Fortune Favors the Felon
Murder is a Premonition Best Served Cold
It's Beginning to Look a Lot Like Murder

A Jailbird in the Vision is Worth Two in the Prison
Great Crimes Read Alike
I Spy With My Psychic Eye Someone Dead
A Vision in Time Saves Nine
There's No Crime Like the Prescient
Fight Fire With Foresight
Something Old, Something New, Something Foretold, Corpse So Blue
Murder Is In the Eye of the Beholder
Between A Vision and A Hard Case
There's More Than One Way to Sense A Killer
A Mental Picture Paints a Thousand Crimes

Cup of Jo Mysteries:
Coffee and Crime
Macchiatos and Murder
Cappuccinos and Corpses
Frappes and Fatalities
Lattes and Lynching
Glaces and Graves
Espresso and Evidence
Americanos and Assault
Doppios and Death
Ristretto and Revenge
Viennas and Vendettas

Madison Kramer Mysteries:
Manuscripts and Murder
Sequels and Serial Killers
Fiction and Felonies

Paranormal Books:
Kiss of Death (Touch of Death Prequel)
Touch of Death (Touch of Death #1)
Stalked by Death (Touch of Death #2)
Face of Death (Touch of Death #3)
Dark Destiny
The Day I Died
Unseen Evil
Evil Unleashed
Replica
Fading Into the Shadows
Into the Fire (Into the Fire #1)
Out of the Ashes (Into the Fire #2)
Up In Flames (Into the Fire #3)

9 7 9 8 8 4 6 5 7 4 6 5 6